SHERLOCK ACADEMY

F.C. Shaw

SHERLOCK ACADEMY

Future House Publishing

Copyright © 2015 by F.C. Shaw

Cover design © 2015 by Future House Publishing

Cover design by Tyler Stott

Interior illustration by Tyler Stott

Interior design by KristiRae Alldredge

ISBN-10: 0-9891253-4-3
ISBN-13: 978-0-9891253-4-5

To Michael,
my own Watson, and comrade
in all our adventures
With love

SA
FINE SLEUTHS

London, England   Friday, 27 June 1931

Rollin E. Wilson:

It is our pleasure to inform you of
your eligibility for the Sherlock
Academy of Fine Sleuths. We believe
you possess the qualities we seek in
fine students. You are invited to a
special orientation at which any
questions you have will be addressed.

Please take advantage of our taxi
service that will pick you up on
Tuesday, 1 July at 8:00 a.m. One adult
may accompany you. We request you bring
only the following item: your favorite
book.

We anticipate making your acquaintance.

An Invitation

The letter arrived by courier during breakfast.

"Go on, Rollie, read it aloud to us." Mrs. Wilson, his mother, nudged his shoulder.

Rollie stared at the letter in his hand, his brown eyes wide with excitement.

"Who would send him mail?" Edward, an older brother, snorted.

"I don't even get mail and I have a girlfriend," Stewart, Edward's twin, added.

"Maybe that's it!" Edward exclaimed, grinning his lopsided smile. "Got a secret girlfriend, Rollie? I'll bet it's Cecily Brighton!"

"I wish I'd get a letter," Lucille, a younger sister, pouted.

"Me too!" Daphne, her twin, chimed.

"Find a boyfriend and you'll get mail," Edward quipped.

Stewart slapped a high-five with his twin. The two teens snickered and elbowed each other.

"Stop it, boys. Let Rollie read it aloud," Mrs. Wilson scolded as she brushed Rollie's sandy-blond hair with her fingers.

Rollie cleared a dry throat unnecessarily. In a high voice common to boys of eleven years, Rollie read the letter aloud. When he was finished, the entire Wilson family started talking at once with high-handed opinions, as was their custom.

"Whoever heard of the Sherlock Academy?"

"Why Tuesday?"

"It's the first of the month."

"I want a letter!"

"Me too!"

"Get a boyfriend."

Amidst all the banter around the breakfast table, Rollie sat silently regarding his hash browns, the only food he ever ate for breakfast. His middle fluttered with butterflies. He felt that flutter when he was excited, like on his birthday, on Christmas day, on the first day of school, and when solving a mystery. Most children his age became very hyper when they felt this flutter in their middles. Perhaps they nagged their parents to no end, or galloped around the house squealing, or did something really naughty like peek at their presents. But in the Wilson household, there was never a need for Rollie to behave this way. Everyone else was louder or more hyper, which, oddly enough, calmed him. Such was the case at the breakfast table laden with pancakes, eggs, and hash browns.

Rollie folded the letter and tucked it in his brown trouser pocket. As he tuned out everyone's comments, he noticed the usual absence of one family member's opinion. He threw a sideways glance at his great-aunt Eileen, who sat primly sipping her tea and holding her tongue. She was thin and of average height, though she always appeared taller because of her upright posture and her tendency to look down her nose at people. She kept her gray hair in a bun atop her head, which also added to her height. Her gray eyes never missed a thing, and the wrinkles on her pale face made her look wise, which she was.

He picked up his fork and poked his hash browns. He scooped up a bit, brought it to his nose, and sniffed. Nope, no use eating at a time like this. Whenever he felt that flutter, his appetite vanished until the excitement resolved. Maybe it was good he got that flutter only three times a year, otherwise he might be even skinnier than he already was.

Rap-rap-rap!

Mr. Wilson rapped his knuckles on the table to get everyone's attention. "Enough, enough! I will lay out the facts and there will be no more talk of this until Tuesday."

Mr. Wilson taught mathematics at the local Regent's College and loved facts as much as he hated speculation. He embodied the role of a professor in his tweed suit, perched spectacles, and straight-combed hair. "Fact: this letter is addressed to Rollie, so it follows that it's no one else's business." He turned a warning eye at Lucille and Daphne who were uncommonly nosey for seven-year-olds. "Fact: the orientation will answer all our questions. Fact: the orientation is not until Tuesday, so there is nothing we can do until Tuesday. Conclusion: this conversation is summed."

Mr. Wilson stood from the table and marched out of the dining room, his morning paper tucked under his arm.

Mrs. Wilson also stood, and smoothed her blue print dress. "Edward, Stewart, don't be late today or you just might get fired. Girls, you have dance lessons at nine. Auntie Ei, if you have any errands, I can drive—"

"No thank you, Eloise." Auntie Ei rose briskly to her feet and swept away quickly despite her eighty-odd years.

"Rollie, your violin lesson is cancelled today. Mrs. Trindle is feeling under the weather." She smoothed his sandy-blond hair and shooed him on his way.

Rollie smiled as the family dispersed. He cared less for violin lessons now than when he first begged his mother for them. He had wanted to play the violin for the sole purpose of mimicking Sherlock Holmes, and enjoyed it to some extent. But he disliked Mrs. Trindle because she smelled stale and flicked the underside of his wrists to "improve the posture," so she said. No violin lesson meant no other plans for the whole day, which spelled freedom until suppertime.

Rollie raced up the stairs, taking them two at a time, pulling himself up by the polished banister. At the end of the hall on the second floor, he mounted twelve more stairs leading to the top of the house. He flew into his watchtower-like bedroom. Being the middle child with no twin did have its advantages: his own bedroom. Though it was the smallest bedroom in the large house, he did not complain, for the house was a gift from Auntie Ei.

Auntie Ei was a lady of property. Long ago, she had passed down the Wilson manor to Rollie's father as an early inheritance on the condition that she would live with them. This meant a crotchety addition to the family and a small room for Rollie. No one understood the reason she chose to live with the family since she was annoyed by all of them—all of them except Rollie. She had a keen interest in him, and a degree of affection for him. When he was old enough to read she had given him his first Sherlock Holmes book, which had planted the thrill of being a detective in Rollie. Despite her partiality toward him she had not been able to secure him a proper bedroom in the house.

But Rollie loved his little room. It had one window overlooking Mr. Crenshaw's garden next door—a great view for spying. Best of all, he was allowed to keep his room any way he wanted.

On the wall nearest the window, he had covered the surface with cork to tack up clues and notes from the cases he solved. On his desk below the window, a telescope peeked through, kept company by a magnifying glass, a spyglass, and binoculars. The rest of his room was filled with boyish delights like a BB rifle, a model airplane, a pennant of his favorite rugby team, and books and books and books.

Rollie plopped down on the navy carpet next to his bookcase. He did not organize his books alphabetically by author or title or even topic like the family's private library downstairs. Instead he organized them by personal rating. Stuck to each shelf, a little label explained his rating system.

The top shelf's label read in his best handwriting *Excellent Books, My Favorites*. The shelf below said *Good Books I Like*. Below that, *Okay Books That Were*

Sort of Good. The last shelf read *Books I Didn't Really Like.* The reason he bothered to keep the books on this last shelf was for appearances only—he hated empty bookshelves. The books on all the shelves constantly shuffled around as he read new ones and added them, or re-read others and revised his rating.

Running his finger along the spines on the top shelf, he read each title lovingly, mental pictures from the stories hugging his mind. Tom Sawyer, Robin Hood, Peter Pan, Lancelot, Sherlock Holmes—

Rollie slid out one of four volumes: *The Return of Sherlock Holmes.* He opened the green hardcover and flipped through the worn pages to "The Adventure of the Empty House." These pages preserved smudges and creases from countless reads. This was his favorite story. He bookmarked it with an original telegram, from Sherlock Holmes to his comrade Doctor John Watson, that Auntie Ei had bought from an antiques auction and given to Rollie. The note gave Watson instructions on where to meet Holmes for a top secret case.

Rollie treasured this telegram, not only because it had been personally written by the great detective, but because he had earned it. A few summers ago Auntie Ei had commissioned Rollie to solve an important mystery for her: to find her sterling silver letter opener that had disappeared. She believed someone in the family had taken it. After questioning the Wilson suspects and searching the premises, Rollie found the letter opener and exposed the culprit, who turned out to be Edward. (He had swiped it from Auntie Ei's desk to etch his initials on the handlebars of his bicycle so it would not get confused with Stewart's matching bicycle.) When Rollie had spotted the telegram behind glass at the antiques auction, he knew exactly which Holmes case it was from. This impressed Auntie Ei so much that she bought it for him as a reward for recovering her silver letter opener, and for being a shrewd Sherlockian. Rollie kept the telegram safely in the Sherlock Holmes book Auntie Ei had given him.

Rollie set aside his book for Tuesday. But . . . He fished out the Sherlock Academy letter from his pocket and read it again.

We request that you bring only the following item and nothing else: your favorite book.

What he had picked out was his favorite *story*; but, when it came down to it, the whole volume was his favorite. Suddenly, he was not sure about bringing a Sherlock Holmes volume. Would every other student bring one also since they were visiting the *Sherlock* Academy? Maybe the school would frown upon that, thinking he brought it in hopes of being accepted.

He scanned the top shelf again. Maybe a different book. He had other favorite books.

No.

Sherlock Holmes remained his ultimate favorite. He revered that detective; Holmes was his hero. His siblings teased him about it.

"He doesn't have any special powers," Edward had pointed out.

"He has the power of deductive reasoning," Rollie had argued.

"Any human can have that," Edward had snorted. "Can he fly or stop a moving train? Does he even have muscles?" Edward had struck a pose in an attempt to show off the sinewy muscles outlining his tall, lean body. "No? Not a hero to me, then."

"He's smarter than Superman," Rollie had insisted.

"What does that matter?"

Rollie did not care about his brother's opinion. He knew Holmes was a worthy hero. Holmes did have muscles, for he was exceptional in boxing and fencing. He could disguise himself, identify all types of cigar and pipe ash, and solve any mystery simply by observing and reasoning. Rollie wanted to be just like him.

Maybe this Sherlock Academy would show him how . . . if that was even what it was all about. No way of knowing until Tuesday. He leaned against his bed and flipped open the volume again. He started reading his favorite case for the umpteenth time just to refresh his memory in case they quizzed him about it on Tuesday.

"Hallo, Rollin Holmes!"

Rollie snapped his head up from his book. "Hallo, Cecily Watson." He hid the book behind his back. "Guess which case I'm reading."

"Good detectives don't guess, they deduce." His best friend, Cecily, bounced into the room, her curly, auburn ponytail bobbing around her neck. She wore a pair of brown slacks too big for her, with the legs rolled up above her ankles and the waist scrunched by a belt to keep them up. She wore a green cardigan with a little patchwork bird on one shoulder. "Your favorite Holmes book is missing from your book-shelf—the green one. I noticed before you closed the book that you were reading at the beginning. The first story in that volume is "The Adventure of the Empty House." Although I should have known from the beginning—it's your favorite. I love "The Adventure of the Dying Detective." Brilliant!"

"Did you steal your brother's trousers again?"

Cecily wrinkled her nose peppered with freckles. "Yeah. Mum still won't buy me my own pair. She says it's not ladylike."

"It's not."

"But I can't climb fences and crawl through bushes and spy in a dress," she pointed out.

"Mr. Crenshaw is in London today, remember?"

"I know. Ooh, which reminds me! The Secret Delivery Case . . ."

"Mrs. Pratcher ordered tulips from Graves Florist," Rollie told her.

"Right." Cecily gave a curt nod. "Only Graves Florist delivers flowers in silver boxes. How do you know she ordered tulips?"

"There was an advertisement in Friday's paper that tulips are half off," said Rollie. "I dug out Mrs. Pratcher's paper from her rubbish bin and noticed she had cut out the advertisement."

"Nice. There's another case wrapped, Holmes." Cecily pulled out a small pocket notebook and a stubby pencil from her back pocket.

Rollie reached over and grabbed the same from his desk. They both flipped through a few pages of notes, then scratched check marks next to *Secret Delivery Case* found at the bottom of a long list of cases they had solved so far that summer.

Cecily cleared her throat. "I have a secret. At least I think it's a secret. I want to tell you because you're my best friend."

Rollie grinned. "I have a secret, too! I think I can tell you. I mean, I wasn't told not to."

Cecily's green eyes sparkled. "You tell me yours first."

"But you mentioned your secret first."

"Oldest to youngest."

"Cecily, I'm only two months older than you."

"It still counts."

"Nope, ladies first."

"We decided I'm not a lady." Cecily shoved her hands deep into her trouser pockets. "Tell me or I'll call you Roly-Poly."

Rollie grimaced, "I hate that. It's not even close to my name. It's *Rollie* with a short *o*. Not *Rolie* with a long *o*."

"Roly-Poly, Roly-Poly—"

"Wait!" Rollie held up his hand. "I know how we can settle this. Let's both tell each other at the same time in code."

They concentrated quietly, and wrote in their notebooks. Then they tore off their papers and exchanged them. They used a common cipher: a long strand of letters with only every third letter used to make words. Quickly they circled every third letter, read the letters, then gaped at each other.

"You got a letter too?" Cecily gasped.

"It came this morning!"

"Mine too!"

"What's your favorite book you're bringing?" Rollie eyed her.

"Um, that is the least of my questions right now. How about this question: what is this all about?" Cecily whipped out her letter from a back pocket. "I've never heard of this Sherlock Academy of Fine Sleuths."

"It's really exciting."

"I'm not so sure yet. It could be a fraud."

Rollie blinked at her. The thought that the Academy might be illegitimate never crossed his mind. He was too enraptured by the idea of becoming a detective like Holmes. "Are you going?"

Cecily shrugged. "I suppose so. There's nothing to lose, but I'm not getting my hopes up."

"Where is the school?"

"The return address says London."

"That's not much to go on. London's huge." Rollie scanned the letter for any more details.

Cecily stood and paced the bedroom. "Jot down the Five Ws."

Rollie flipped to a new page in his pocket notebook. He listed down the page WHO, WHAT, WHERE, WHEN, and WHY. "Who is it?" he mumbled, scribbling. He chewed on his pencil.

"What is it?" Cecily stopped, then resumed pacing.

"Where is it? When does this Academy start?"

Cecily stopped pacing and narrowed her eyes. "Why do they want us?"

Rollie read his letter, "*We believe you possess the qualities we seek in fine students.*"

"What qualities?"

Rollie nodded his agreement and jotted that question down. "Tuesday seems like forever away."

"Four days if you count today."

Rollie shook his head. "Let's not. Let's say three days. It's more bearable."

Cecily nodded. "Very well. Three days until we clear up this mystery."

Taxied Away

Dinner with the Wilsons was more chaotic than breakfast because everyone wanted to share about the day. Usually Mr. Wilson told a funny anecdote about one of his students. Stewart rambled on about his girlfriend, Alice, whose father he and Edward worked for. Meanwhile, Edward jealously badgered his brother about having a girlfriend, and stated that he wanted to find a new job. Lucille and Daphne giggled about dance lessons. Auntie Ei never said a word. Mrs. Wilson refereed the dinner table, nudged Rollie to eat more, laughed at Mr. Wilson's story, and shushed the twins when she thought their turns were up. As for Rollie, he usually sat quietly taking in everything, but not eating much, being a picky eater.

But tonight was different. It was Monday night, which meant Tuesday came at dawn. For the first time in a while, the family conversation focused on Rollie and the Sherlock Academy orientation.

"Tomorrow's the day, son," Mr. Wilson stated plainly in between bites of his roast beef. "Fact: it's supposed to be a beautiful day. And it's supposed to be Tuesday all day." He winked.

Rollie appreciated his father's silly sense of humor.

"What time are you leaving, son?"

"Eight o'clock—"

"Eight o'clock!" Edward exclaimed. "Wait a minute. Just because that's the same time I have to leave for work doesn't mean I'm taking Roly-Poly with me. I have—"

"Edward, calm down," Mrs. Wilson cut in, buttering her roll. "We didn't ask that of you, did we?"

"I'm just throwing it out there before you get any ideas," Edward said, shoveling mashed potatoes into his mouth.

Stewart swallowed his bite of carrots. "Good job, Ed. Way to think ahead."

Mrs. Wilson dabbed her mouth with a napkin. "We haven't decided who is going with Rollie."

"Is someone supposed to go with him?" Mr. Wilson glanced over his spectacles at her.

"Well, you didn't think he'd go alone to who-knows-where?"

"Roly-Poly's never been anywhere alone, have you?" Edward teased.

"I have too!" Rollie suddenly felt defensive. "I go to school alone every day."

Stewart chuckled. "Good comeback, Rollie."

Mr. Wilson took off his spectacles and gnawed on one of the ends thoughtfully. "I can't go. I've got Mathematics 102."

"I will accompany him." Auntie Ei stood from the table decidedly, and loomed over them. "Be ready at the door at eight o'clock sharp, Rollin." With that, she vacated the dining room.

A few moments of unusual silence followed as the family gaped after the old woman.

Mrs. Wilson blinked. "Bless her."

Mr. Wilson grunted. "Fact: she's unpredictable."

Edward and Stewart slapped high-fives, relieved they did not have to take Rollie.

Lucille and Daphne giggled.

And Rollie frowned as he felt that usual flutter in his middle again.

* * * *

As expected, Rollie's sleepless night was wrought with anxiety. Along with reducing his appetite, that flutter in his middle never preceded a decent night's sleep. However difficult falling asleep was, somehow

Rollie always woke up in the morning, which meant he had at some point indeed fallen asleep.

Such was the case Tuesday morning when he found himself waking up to his red alarm clock ringing. He clicked it off and jumped out of bed. He yanked open all the drawers in his dresser in a sudden panic, for he had no idea what to wear to the orientation. On a day-to-day basis he put little thought into what he wore, mainly because his wardrobe was far from exciting—all hand-me-downs from Edward and Stewart.

Rollie pulled out a pair of navy trousers sporting grass stains on the knees; he stuffed them back in the drawer. He shook out a gray wrinkled shirt and noticed a button missing. He kept pulling out clothes and for the first time noticed how hard he was on his wardrobe, for it was riddled with rips, stains, snags, and frays. And all his pockets were stuffed with odds and ends like paper clips, candy wrappers, pebbles, and pencil shavings, to name a few. He felt a little embarrassed until he remembered that Sherlock Holmes rarely took notice of his wardrobe, for he was much too consumed with clues to worry about clothes. Rollie decided he was the same way. Still, it wouldn't do to go to the orientation with disheveled clothes. Mr. Wilson was fond of telling Rollie that "a careless appearance reflects a careless mind." Maybe his father was right. What if Rollie was dismissed from the orientation because his clothes were wrinkled?

His mother poked her head into the room. "Good morning, my Rollie, are you excited?"

"What should I wear, Mum?"

Clearly panic showed in his eyes and a quiver vibrated in his voice because Mrs. Wilson flitted into the room. "Don't worry. I know just the thing." She rummaged through his closet and pulled out his best blue blazer. "Wear the blue slacks and a collared shirt. Oh, and a tie. You should look your best, I think." She dug a hand into the outer pockets of the blazer and found a fistful of trash. She gave him an amused look before leaving the bedroom.

Within ten minutes Rollie was completely dressed and groomed. He grabbed *The Return of Sherlock Holmes* and headed downstairs. Standing beside the front door, Auntie Ei leaned on her umbrella for support. She took great care in her appearance, and was dressed nicely in a lilac floral dress, matching hat, and white gloves. She smelled of lavender.

"Good morning, Auntie."

"Good morning, Rollin. Do you have your favorite book?"

Rollie held it up. "Think it's okay to bring a Sherlock Holmes volume?"

"Absolutely. Why not?"

"Don't you think a lot of the other kids will bring Sherlock Holmes?"

"Whoever said there would be other children?"

"Cecily is coming."

"Is she bringing Sherlock Holmes too?"

Rollie shrugged. "I don't know."

"Well, there you have it. Straighten your tie. Don't forget your manners."

"Yes, Auntie."

Ding-Dong!

Rollie jumped. His heart skipped and his middle flipped into double fluttering. Both the parlor grandfather clock and the front doorbell chimed at the same time.

Auntie Ei opened the door to a short, squat man in a bowler hat and long, black coat.

"Morning, ma'am. I'm 'ere for a Rollin E. Wilson," he greeted, reading the name from an index card.

"We're ready. Rollin!" Auntie Ei called as she stepped onto the porch.

"Lady Wilson, let me 'elp you into the cab." Rollie blushed a bit when he remembered too late that he should have offered to help Aunt Ei. The driver escorted Auntie Ei by the arm to a black horse-drawn cab, much like the ones popular in London in the late

1800s. It balanced on two wheels and was hitched to a single chestnut horse.

Auntie Ei seemed not the least surprised, but Rollie gaped at it.

"You don't have an automobile?" he asked.

"No, lad, this is our taxi service." The driver opened for them two little doors that swung aside like window shutters, and helped Auntie Ei into the cab. "This 'ere's called a hansom and it's the Academy's official transportation. It's just like one of the hansoms—"

"Sherlock Holmes may have ridden in!" exclaimed Rollie.

"Rollin, it is very rude to interrupt. Get in," Auntie Ei ordered.

A little embarrassed, Rollie leaped into the hansom and sat on the edge of the cushion. He peered out the little round window in the back. The driver climbed up to his perch above in the back, flicked the reins, and got the cab moving down the street.

"Auntie, have you ever been in one of these?"

"To answer would be to reveal how old I am. A lady never reveals her age, nor should little boys raise the question." She paused, a tight smile playing on her wrinkled face. "Perhaps I have been in one before."

Rollie expected to stop a few doors down to pick up Cecily, but the cab passed by her house. He spotted a similar hansom and driver stopped at Cecily's door.

Within twenty minutes, they drove south into London. They turned down several busy streets. Cars honked at the antique cab, but this did not seem to bother the driver or the horse. At first Rollie knew where they were, for he visited London with his mother almost every Saturday to check the post and do a bit of shopping. As the hansom turned onto smaller streets, Rollie lost his bearings, for they drove through a part of London he had never visited. He wondered if the driver was deliberately taking them on a confusing route.

Rollie assumed correctly, for as they turned out of a small alley he suddenly knew where they were. He recognized Regent's Park and spotted Regent's College where his father taught. He wondered if maybe he had passed by Sherlock Academy without knowing it every time he visited Regent's College. He vowed to be more observant like Cecily in the future.

Soon the driver pulled on the reins to stop the cab, and hopped off his high perch to open the doors facing the horse's rear.

"May I help you down, Aunt Ei?" Rollie asked quickly, remembering his manners.

A brief, small smile played across her face as she accepted his offer and let him help her out of the cab, but she seemed relieved to take the arm of the driver who escorted her down the sidewalk. Rollie stopped and stared up at the tall, red-brick building with rows of windows and one door. A flat roof with a chain-link fence crowned the four-story building.

"Rollie!"

Rollie whirled around to find Cecily hopping out of her horse-drawn hansom. She was alone. She smoothed down her dress and rushed up to him, excitement in her green eyes.

"Have you ever been in one of those cabs?" she asked him.

"No, but I really felt like—"

"Sherlock Holmes! I know! Rollie, look where we are!"

Rollie looked up again at the drab building. Posted above the mailbox, next to the front door, was the building's address:

221 Baker Street.

Just Like Old Times

"Is this really 221 Baker Street?" Rollie asked as he and Cecily caught up with Auntie Ei.

"Of course it is, Rollin, you can see for yourself on the wall." Auntie Ei ushered him toward the front double doors.

"So this is really where Sherlock Holmes lived?"

"At one point in his life," a woman's voice from inside answered as they bustled into the building.

They stood in a hall with a flight of stairs ascending before them, both carpeted in green. An antique gas lamp hung from the ceiling, lending dull light on the dark-paneled walls and doors. A woman wearing a light pink tie, a brown skirt, and a matching blazer stood at the foot of the staircase. Her mousey-brown hair was pulled back in a tight bun, and her posture was rigid. She drummed her fingers on the dark wood banister.

"You will recall that Holmes's original residence was burned by his nemesis Moriarty when Holmes fled London in 1893. It was then rebuilt, and Holmes took up residency here when he returned from his hiatus after defeating Moriarty. Welcome. Orientation is about to commence. Follow me." She turned to her left and led them down the hallway to a door at the end. She opened the door and marched into a small room that looked like it had once been someone's flat. Cozy couches, armchairs, and end tables furnished the room. "Please find a seat."

The room boasted other boys and girls and a few adults sitting on couches and armchairs. All the children looked to be around Rollie's age of eleven years old. There were four other boys and four other girls, making an even ten with himself and Cecily. Auntie Ei herded Rollie and Cecily over to a couch.

A man entered the room and took his place behind a podium—a formal gesture compared to the informal seating arrangements. He wore a brown suit and light pink tie to match the militant woman who guarded the door. He was very tall and thin, and topped with a receding hairline. Subtle bags drooped beneath his keen eyes, yet he did not appear tired. His sharp facial features—hawk-like nose, square chin, and prominent forehead—were strikingly similar to those of the great detective Holmes.

"Welcome to the Sherlock Academy of Fine Sleuths. I am Headmaster Sullivan P. Yardsly. I am very happy to see you all here. Let's not waste any time and get right down to business. What is the business at hand, you ask? Well . . ." He presented a white poster from behind the podium. On the poster were listed down one side: WHO, WHAT, WHERE, WHEN, WHY, and HOW.

Rollie elbowed Cecily, and she smiled back.

"WHO!" Headmaster Yardsly boomed, causing everyone to jump, especially a plump boy chewing gum. Back at a normal pitch, Yardsly continued, "We are searching for students with heightened skills in deductive reasoning with the potential to be great detectives. This brings me to our next question:

"WHAT!" Again Headmaster Yardsly made everyone jump. A little girl with golden ringlets clapped her hands over her ears. "As you know, this school is named the Sherlock Academy of Fine Sleuths in honor of the finest sleuth who ever worked in London. We seek to train future detectives to follow in the footsteps of our dear Holmes." Here he paused to take a sip of water that he procured from behind the podium.

"WHERE!" Yardsly still caught them off guard. "You are currently sitting in an old flat in an exact replica of the most famous building ever located on Baker Street, or in London, in my opinion. Yes, this is *the* address where Sherlock Holmes and his dear comrade Doctor John Watson resided.

"WHEN! Classes are Monday through Friday, nine to four. We provide housing for students here, which you might find convenient. We include basic academia to keep up with standard education, but our main focus is teaching skills to create future detectives." He paused and everyone braced for his next shout.

"WHY! With the rate of crime increasing and the state of Europe growing more uncertain, we should invest in future crime-fighters. A number of our graduates join Scotland Yard, the Metropolitan Police, or open private investigation agencies." He took another sip.

"HOW! Students will live and study here. They will complete a four-year basic training. What is that basic training called, you ask? We call it *The Sign of the Four*." He chuckled over his reference to Holmes's case.

Rollie and Cecily chuckled at the inside Sherlockian joke.

Headmaster Yardsly continued, "After completing the four-year training, students have several options they can choose from. They can return to normal schooling like secondary school or college, or enroll in Scotland Yard's Apprentice Detective Program. I hope that answers all your questions." He took another sip of his water and blinked at the children around the room.

Everyone sat very still and stared at the headmaster, except for a grandfatherly man who wrapped his arm around a skinny bug-eyed boy.

"Good. If there are no questions, I would like to ask all the potential students to please follow Ms. Katherine E. Yardsly—my colleague and sister. Please bring your favorite book with you."

Rollie and Cecily bounced up from the couch. Auntie Ei yanked on Rollie's sleeve.

"Rollin, trust your instincts," she whispered, and gave him a curt nod.

Rollie caught up with Cecily at the door and followed the rest of the children down the hallway. Had they all received letters like he had? Would all of them be accepted into the school? A further question nagged him: how did this school even know about him, know about his love for detecting and for the great Holmes? He hoped more answers would come from Ms. Katherine E. Yardsly.

"Here we are," Ms. Yardsly announced more loudly than necessary. She opened a door off the hallway and led the children inside.

They found themselves in what had once been a small flat, but now it appeared to serve as a library. The walls displayed bookcases touching all the way to the ceiling, and a few ladders rested against them to give access to the tippy-top shelves. One brown leather armchair and adjoining end table with a green banker's lamp stood as the only other furniture, for there was no more room with so many bookcases. The unusual thing about this library was a minor detail: the books on the shelves lay on their sides, stacked atop each other, as opposed to standing on end side by side like other libraries' books.

"Take a good look around, children," Ms. Yardsly commanded loudly. She planted herself in the center of the room and spread her arms wide. "Any comments?" She looked from one child to the other.

Rollie raised his hand, unsure how to address her.

"Yes, Rollin E. Wilson?"

"Why do you stack the books vertically instead of lining them up side by side?"

"You'll soon know the reason. Children, you must decide right now if you want to commit to Sherlock Academy. You will show me your answer with one of two actions. If you wish to attend, simply place your favorite book on the end table. If you do not wish to attend, simply hug your book to yourself."

The children looked around at each other, unsure what to decide. What a small gesture for so grand a decision!

A round little boy about Rollie's age asked, "Can I ask my parents first? I don't know what they want me to do."

"No, this is *your* choice."

"I don't think I'll like this school," the little girl with golden ringlets muttered as she hugged her book and stepped back against the door.

"Very well. No hard feelings. You made the right decision for yourself," Ms. Yardsly stated very matter-of-factly. "Quickly, children, quickly."

One dark-haired boy whose pants were a bit short stepped forward and slapped his book on the end table. "This is all very mysterious. I like it."

Rollie agreed. He really wanted to join in a mystery, but he knew so little about it. He wished he had more information . . . but then it would not be a mystery. He felt a flutter in his middle, a good flutter. Nope, if he wanted to be a detective, he must not second-guess his instincts.

Rollin, trust your instincts, he heard Auntie Ei's encouraging words in his head.

He placed his beloved Sherlock Holmes volume on top of the other boy's book. He sneaked a glance at the other title: *The Hound of the Baskervilles.*

Cecily came up behind him and stacked her book, *The Casebook of Sherlock Holmes,* on top of his. Another girl with little spectacles set down her book, *A Study in Scarlet.* So far they were the only four. The other six children stood by the door, books pressed close to their chests. Rollie wondered what their titles were. He stepped nearer and read a few of their spines: *Peter Pan, The Wind in the Willows, Alice in Wonderland, The Swiss Family Robinson* . . . He strained to read the last two. *Peter Pan* again, and . . . *Aesop's Fables.* No Sherlock Holmes. Hmm . . .

"Children, you may return to your adults right down the hall," Ms. Yardsly instructed. "Except you four. Stay a moment." She waited until the six had vacated the room, then she scooped up the favorite books on the end table, and headed toward a wall of bookshelves. Randomly, she put each book on top of a different stack. Then she spun back around to the children. "Could you find your books again?"

Rollie glanced at Cecily. The other boy and girl regarded each other. They all shrugged. That seemed too easy. They could see their books on the different shelves. They all nodded.

"Rollin E. Wilson."

"Yes, Ms. Yardsly?"

"You asked the reason we stack our books instead of lining them up beside each other." Ms. Yardsly pulled up her sleeve to read her wristwatch. "Three, two, one." She gave a curt nod.

Instantly, an extraordinary thing happened. Rollie jumped as he looked at the bookcase in front of him.

With a whooshing and thumping sound much like wind banging shutters, the bookshelves slid aside or dropped or rose. One shelf divider slid to the right, pushing a stack of books with it. The shelf the stack rested on suddenly gave way like a trap door, plopping the stack of books down to the shelf below it. Another shelf divider slid that stack to the left to make way for the shelf below to rise and propel a new stack of books up through the trap door. The new stack of books rested on the shelf where the first stack of books had previously been.

This was just one example of the dizzying motion. The entire library rearranged as every single shelf on every bookcase relocated every single stack of books. So quickly did the library change, the children practically gasped for breath. As suddenly as it had begun, it stopped.

Ms. Yardsly turned to the four astounded children and asked, "Now could you find your book?"

They stared at her, then at the bookshelves that were anything but recognizable.

"You are welcome to figure out the pattern of the shelves and find your book while attending the Academy," Ms. Yardsly told them. As she turned to leave, she added, "The library is on its own timer. It rearranges every twelve hours."

"So there is a distinct pattern to how they move?" Cecily asked, fascinated.

"Why on earth would you want a library like that?" the dark-haired boy wondered aloud. "You'd never be able to find anything!"

"Yes, you would, if you knew the pattern," Cecily argued.

"It's a great strategy," Rollie added. "It's one way to make sure you stay committed. You wouldn't drop out unless you didn't really care about your book."

"Is that true?" the girl wearing spectacles asked.

Ms. Yardsly ignored their questions. She led them down the hallway to the room where the adults waited. Rollie barely caught a glimpse of Headmaster Yardsly and Auntie Ei re-entering the room, and wondered where they had gone together. Inside they found only Auntie Ei, a petite dark-haired woman, and Headmaster Sullivan P. Yardsly in the room. The headmaster stepped behind his podium as Auntie Ei took her seat on the couch. When the children and Ms. Yardsly entered, Yardsly shot his hands up in the air.

"Hooray for our new students!" he beamed. "I'm so excited to enroll you. I believe you are very gifted children. I look forward to training you into fine detectives. What did you think of the Rearranging Library? Cecily A. Brighton?"

"I think it's brilliant!" Cecily exclaimed.

"It's very mysterious," the dark-haired boy muttered.

Headmaster Yardsly pointed a slender, delicate finger at him. "That's the word I sought, Eliot S. Tildon. Anyone else? What did you think, Tabbitha A. Smith?"

"I suppose it's interesting, but I definitely want my book back."

"Rollin E. Wilson?"

"It's very clever. I mean to solve the pattern."

"That's the spirit! Students, these are for you."

Headmaster Yardsly reached behind his podium and brought out a stack of four broad boxes. He presented each student with one.

"Welcome to Sherlock Academy, sleuths!"

Shakespeare's Secret

The cab bounced along the road. Auntie Ei sat stiff and proper, occasionally glancing out a little side window. Rollie sat snugly between her and Cecily. Since the hansom was intended for two passengers, the three of them sat cozily close together. Both Rollie and Cecily balanced broad rectangular boxes wrapped with brown paper and string on their laps. Little tags with instructions dangled from the string: *New Student Admissions Package. Do not open until safely home.*

"I wonder if this is anything like the admissions package I got in the mail a few weeks ago," Cecily wondered aloud.

"You got an admissions package from them already?" Rollie asked.

"No, not from them. It's from the all-girls boarding school Mum is thinking of sending me to. Let's hope she changes her mind and lets me go to this school. This one is much more exciting."

"What was in that admissions package?"

"Forms and forms and more forms. All boring. Just paperwork that had too much print. I'll bet this one just has forms and papers for our parents." Cecily rolled her eyes and stuck out her tongue.

Rollie shrugged. He hoped that this admissions package would be more interesting than a bunch of paperwork, but there was no way to tell. Maybe Cecily was right.

Auntie Ei glanced at them, then back at the window. "Hardly, my dear boy. Hardly."

Rollie studied her and thought he spied a smile tugging on the corners of her mouth. "Do you know what's in here, Auntie?"

"Rollin, how would I possibly know what is in that box?"

Rollie did not answer her. The deliberate looks she gave and odd things she said made Rollie wonder if Auntie Ei knew more than she appeared to.

"Auntie, do you think Mum and Dad will let me go to this school?"

"They'll have to. You need to get your book back."

"They might not think that's a good enough reason." Rollie had a sudden thought and had to stifle a gasp. He remembered he had left the Holmes telegram inside his book. He did not tell Auntie Ei this, as he was sure she would scold him for being careless with such a prized item. He hoped the Rearranging Library would keep it safe.

"It is most certainly a good enough reason, which reminds me, Rollin. You will have to cancel your violin lessons with Mrs. Trindle once you start at the Academy. However, I strongly urge you to practice your violin when you return home for weekends."

"Should I take it with me?" asked Rollie.

"No need. You will be too busy with your detective lessons."

The driver pulled up the reins and hopped down from the cab. He opened the doors. "'Ere we are, miss. Number 18 Primrose Lane." He tipped his bowler hat and helped Cecily out of the hansom.

"Bye, Rollie! I'll see you tomorrow. It was nice to see you again, Lady Wilson." Cecily waved and skipped down her front walkway.

"She is a clever girl," said Auntie Ei. "Though I don't approve of her wearing trousers. Thank goodness her mother made her wear a dress to orientation—that is only proper."

With a flick of the reins, the driver guided the horse two houses down, and stopped. "Number 22 Primrose Lane." He escorted Auntie Ei out. "Good afternoon, Lady Wilson. Lad."

Auntie Ei marched up the hedge-lined walkway and through the front double doors. Rollie scampered after her, clutching his box under his arm. They entered just as the grandfather clock in the parlor struck noon. Rollie thought it was later than that, for he felt like he had been gone all day.

They had barely taken their coats off when Mr. Wilson barged through the front door. During the summer, he finished teaching his courses by late noon and made it a point to be home for lunch. He hung his briefcase and fedora on the hall tree and dabbed his brow with his handkerchief.

"Fact: it's a bit warm today. I hope Cook has some fresh lemonade. Oh, Auntie Ei, Rollie, how was your morning at, uh, what's the name of it again?"

"Sherlock Academy." Auntie Ei stated, annoyed at her nephew's forgetfulness.

"Dad, they have this library that—"

"Rest easy, son. Let's get some lunch, then you can tell Mum and me all about it." Mr. Wilson led them through the house to the back porch, where lunch waited.

"Rollie! Auntie Ei! You're back just in time," Mrs. Wilson exclaimed, kissing Rollie's forehead. "Lunch is ready."

The family, minus Edward and Stewart who ate their lunch at the shop, scooted around the small

38

table laden with cold meat sandwiches and lemonade. Lucille and Daphne tried to start the conversation by recounting their mother-daughter tea that morning, but Auntie Ei would not allow it.

"For goodness' sake, you two, stop giggling over your ridiculous tea," the old woman snapped. "The conversation today will be about Rollin and his new school. Rollin, do you have the admissions package?"

Lucille and Daphne bent their heads together and continued to titter, not being the least bit offended by Auntie Ei's insult.

Unused to being the center of attention, Rollie hesitantly reached down beside his chair and hoisted up the box. "Should I open it?" He gave the box a gentle shake and heard a few objects clunk around inside.

Auntie Ei nodded. "You are safely home, are you not? Open it!"

Rollie slipped off the string, then peeled off the paper—slowly at first, then more feverishly, the way he opened presents. A box, as he had expected. A long envelope addressed to his parents rested atop the lid. He handed it to his father.

Mr. Wilson pushed his spectacles farther up his nose and ripped open the envelope. He slipped out a folded piece of paper and flapped it open. He cleared his throat, but read it silently. His brow furrowed deeper with every line he read.

"What does it say, Peter?" Mrs. Wilson asked. "Read it aloud."

"It's all very . . ." he stammered, searching for the right word.

"Mysterious?" Rollie ventured.

"Yes, exactly, son. Mysterious."

Rollie beamed. He had hoped for just that when he opened the package.

Mr. Wilson cleared his throat again and read:

"*To the Parents of Rollin E. Wilson,*

It gives us great pleasure to admit your talented son to our esteemed Academy. We have no doubt he will thrive here and be an asset to our institution, as well as to all of England someday.

Rollin E. Wilson has been specially selected from students all over the United Kingdom to participate in our program that will enhance and utilize his fine abilities in detection.

Classes begin 1 August—we take short summer holidays! Rollin has the option of boarding at our school or commuting during the week. An anonymous benefactor will be paying for his tuition.

Enclosed you will find Rollin's class schedule. He must know his class schedule by the first day of school.

With all due respect and gratitude,
Headmaster Sullivan P. Yardsly
Sherlock Academy of Fine Sleuths"

Mr. Wilson took off his spectacles and chewed on one of the ends. "There you have it. The fact still remains that this is all very . . . mysterious."

"I don't quite understand," Mrs. Wilson spoke up. "Would Rollie attend this school in place of or in addition to his regular schooling?"

"In place of," Auntie Ei said. "Headmaster Yardsly explained that they carry on regular instruction in mathematics and science and such, but they also instruct them in detective skills."

"It's like an apprenticeship for an occupation," Mr. Wilson added. "Rollie, would you like to attend this school?"

"Yes, Dad, I really want to."

"Eloise?" Mr. Wilson turned to his wife.

"Can it be trusted as a school of quality education?" Mrs. Wilson asked doubtfully.

"Absolutely!" Auntie Ei exclaimed in a tone of offense.

Rollie held his breath, itching to hear his parents' consent, itching to open the box on his lap. He observed his parents communicating with their eyes, as they often did before declaring a decision aloud.

"Very well, son, open the box," his father shrugged again.

Rollie gripped the edges and slowly pulled up the lid. He stared a moment at the large, very thick, hardback, leather-bound book lying in the box. "*The Complete Works of William Shakespeare,*" he said in a deadpan tone, almost too low to be heard. If he had not been so mystified, he might have groaned aloud in disappointment. He loved books, but he had plenty of those. The family library housed all of Shakespeare's works already; He didn't need his own personal copy. He had hoped to find a class schedule or spy gadgets in the box. Wait—he shook the book again and heard several somethings shift around.

"Rollin, do not judge a book by its cover," Auntie Ei told him sternly. "Open it."

He opened the cover. A deep hole had been carved through the pages of the book. In that hole lay five random items. One by one, Rollie showed them to his family and set them on the table:

One large skeleton key with 0900A engraved on its stem.

One smoking pipe (resembling what Holmes would have smoked) with 1130F inscribed on the side.

One ballpoint pen with 1300H typed on the cap.

One small vial of what appeared to be dust labeled with 1030D.

One red ball cap embroidered with 1400G on the brim.

"All of that was in the book?" Mrs. Wilson asked, surprised.

"It's a hollow book, Mum. See?" Rollie held up the book to show her the cavity carved into it. He noticed the inside cover marked *Personal Property of Rollin E. Wilson*. "It's a great way to keep your stuff secret because everybody thinks it's a book."

"Unless you show it to your whole family," whispered Daphne to Lucille. Rollie still heard her and made a personal note not to put anything important in it.

"Fact: that's an ingenious method for keeping your property private," Mr. Wilson stated, a twinkle of excitement in his brown eyes. He reached over and picked up the smoking pipe, analyzing it closely. "This is a model—a nice replica of a pipe, but a model. I daresay I hope they don't teach you to smoke a pipe at this new school."

"I'll never smoke!" Rollie exclaimed. "Remember that time Edward snuck a cigar and tried it out? You made him smoke the whole box to teach him a lesson. He got so sick!"

Rollie's parents laughed, and Auntie Ei cracked a tight smile.

"He looked so green!" Mrs. Wilson chuckled. "The punishment fit the crime."

"Rollin, read us your class schedule," Auntie Ei cut in.

Rollie searched the inside of the book again. "There is no class schedule."

"But the letter said the class schedule was enclosed," Auntie Ei insisted.

"Nothing in here but those objects." Rollie tipped the book upside-down, hoping an explanation would fall from it.

"It certainly is mysterious." Mrs. Wilson poured Lucille more lemonade. "Perhaps a little too mysterious for comfort."

Auntie Ei shook her head. "That's the way it must be. It does little good to merely *teach* students how to solve mysteries. They must *apply* their skills to realistic situations. I guarantee that this class schedule is just the beginning. It's good for him. Hopefully he'll be a full-fledged detective someday." She opened the *Daily Telegraph* newspaper and perused it. "God knows we need more intelligent detectives these days with Herr Zilch still at large."

Rollie glanced at the headline of the newspaper: "Murder in Piccadilly Circus Linked to London's Notorious Villain Herr Zilch." This piece of news did not surprise him, for the newspapers were always reporting crimes involving the mysterious criminal Herr Zilch. Rollie knew very little about him beyond the newspapers' reports, but Auntie Ei seemed to have a vested interest in him.

Right now Rollie had more mysterious things to draw his attention. He stared at the singular items on the table. *Enclosed you will find Rollin's class schedule.* How were these items related to his classes? What did these numbers and letters on each item signify? That flutter of excitement grew in his middle as the mystery grew in his mind.

Timetables and Such

"I have never been more relieved in all my life," Cecily exclaimed.

Up in Rollie's watchtower bedroom, she and Rollie sat at his desk under the window. They took turns peeping through the telescope, then through the binoculars, watching Mr. Crenshaw in his garden below. The elderly gentleman lounged in his favorite chair under a willow tree, and sorted through his briefcase. The angle was just right, allowing the two sleuths to read the papers he shuffled through. Periodically he sipped his coffee.

While he had moved in next door only six months ago, Mr. Crenshaw had wasted no time in being neighborly to the Wilsons. He always exchanged friendly words with Rollie's father, and sent little gifts of flowers, chocolates, and fruit to the family on special holidays like Valentine's and Easter. The first time he caught Rollie and Cecily spying on him he chuckled and gave them a wink. Rollie wondered if he sometimes purposely sat in his back garden to give the young detectives some spying practice. He always seemed amused by them. A few times he had invited Rollie and Cecily to his house to discuss detective work over tea, for he shared their same interest in mysteries.

"I mean, just a few weeks ago I was worried about going to this all-girls boarding school in Newcastle," Cecily continued. "Now I'm going to this brilliant school where I get to do what I like best. I get to go with my best friend, too. How did my luck change?"

"I have no idea," Rollie mumbled. "I was sure your mum wouldn't let you go. What made her say yes?"

Cecily focused the binoculars. "A few things. First, I can board there. Also the tuition is *way* cheaper than the Newcastle school. And I begged a lot."

"How much is the tuition?" Rollie heard Mr. Crenshaw ring a little bell. In response, his young, brassy-haired secretary emerged from the house, a notepad and pen in her hands, her high-heels *clippety-clopping* across the patio.

"Didn't you read your letter?"

"Someone is paying for my tuition," Rollie told her. "Who?"

"I don't know. An anonymous benefactor."

Cecily looked at him. "That's interesting. Sure it's not your family?"

"They couldn't be anonymous, even if they tried. My family can't keep anything a secret."

"Good point. Who else knows about you and the school?"

"I have no idea," Rollie shrugged.

"You know what I wonder about, Rollie?" Cecily put down the binoculars. "How did the Academy know about our skills as detectives?"

"Do you think Mrs. Simmons had something to do with it?" Rollie wondered.

He had thought a lot about his past teacher. One day in April she had caught him making notes in his journal about Anthony Green, who he suspected of stealing the class candy jar. Rollie had been afraid that Mrs. Simmons would punish him for those notes, but instead she encouraged him to pursue solving the case, just not during math. After that she had several conversations with him about his love for Sherlock Holmes and his love for solving mysteries. Rollie had mentioned that Cecily also enjoyed the same hobby. On the last day of final exams, Mrs. Simmons had added one more exam not typically given to ten year old students. The exam contained twenty unusual and complicated questions. Although Rollie had felt good about his answers, he never saw the results.

"I was thinking the same thing!" Cecily gasped. "What were some of the questions on that exam?"

"*If you are looking at a rainbow, where is the sun located?*" Rollie cited. "There was something about a chess position, too."

"Oh! And there were a bunch of questions where you had to predict the pattern or something."

"I wonder if that was a test to find students with certain skills— like what the Academy was looking for." Rollie squinted through the telescope. "Mr. Crenshaw is looking at blueprints to a building."

Cecily picked up the binoculars again. "What building?"

"I'm looking for an address."

Cecily handed Rollie the binoculars and he quickly twisted the knob to focus them. "His fingers are in the way. Don't you think it's funny that he always wears gloves? Even in the summer?"

"Sort of, although I know gentlemen are fond of wearing gloves." Cecily leaned over the desk to better see out the window.

"Maybe something's wrong with his hands." Rollie set the binoculars down. "I've never seen his hands without gloves."

"He put the blueprints away and is looking at an invoice." Cecily pressed her right eye to the telescope.

"Wait, he's spotted us." Rollie watched Mr. Crenshaw glance up at his bedroom window and smile.

Mr. Crenshaw scribbled on a piece of paper, then held it up for the two sleuths to read: *Tea in twenty minutes?* Rollie and Cecily nodded back, to which Mr. Crenshaw gave them a wave and went back to sorting through his briefcase.

"What do you want to work on for twenty minutes?" Cecily stood up from the desk.

"How about our *class schedule*," Rollie intonated these last words with sarcasm. He loved mysteries, but hated ones that stumped him for too long. A week had passed, and those items in the hollow book still baffled him.

Cecily sighed. "I did figure one thing out: We have the same class schedule."

Rollie socked her gently in the shoulder. "Ha, ha. Elementary, my dear Watson."

"What information is on a normal class schedule?"

Rollie grabbed his notepad and pencil stub. "Name of the class. Name of the professor teaching the class. Time of the class. The room the class is in. That's what are on those college class schedules my dad has. Have you come up with anything?"

"Maybe each item has something to do with its class."

"I thought of that too." Rollie flipped through his notepad to a list. "The cap could represent P.E."

Rollie and Cecily tried to assign the items to classes: the vial of dust for science, and the pen for writing. But when they came to the pipe and the key, they got stumped again. Rollie ventured a bit of creativity, saying the key could be for history according to the metaphorical idea that the past is the key to the future. Cecily laughed that the pipe could be for home economics. In the end, they agreed that their guesses were not concrete enough.

"Any student could interpret these objects any way," said Cecily.

Rollie picked up the key and studied it. "Let's go after these numbers and letters. They could be the course ID."

"What do you mean?"

"College courses have titles and numbers and letters," Rollie explained. "My dad teaches math course numbers 102A and 102B."

"That makes sense!" Cecily picked up the pipe. "So this class is course number 1130F. It has something to do with pipes. If that's the case, then we can't do anything more until we go to school and look up their class courses. How can we know what class is 1130F?"

Rollie frowned. He remembered the Academy expected him to arrive the first day of school and know his class schedule. Was he missing something else? Were his detective skills not as fine as he had come to believe?

"I don't think that's it either," he said.

"I think that's it," Cecily countered. She stood up and stretched. "Until we go, we can't know anything more. Let's go over to Mr. Crenshaw's."

Rollie followed her out of the bedroom and downstairs. They headed next door and entered the back garden through a side gate they had used before. As they entered the garden, they spotted Mr. Crenshaw still sitting in his chair under the willow tree. He stood in greeting and smiled at them.

He might have been a tall man, but his height was hard to tell because he stood with a stoop and shuffled around on slightly bent knees. He was nearly bald, except for tufts of white hair encircling his head. His face was lined with wrinkles and heavy bags drooped beneath his eyes. Rollie guessed he had to be older than Auntie Ei.

"Good day, detectives," Mr. Crenshaw greeted, beckoning them to sit in two chairs across from him. A small table next to him was laid with tea and biscuits. "What case are you working on today?"

"We're decoding our class schedule," Rollie told him.

"For Sherlock Academy," added Cecily.

Mr. Crenshaw's white eyebrows shot up. "You've been accepted at Sherlock Academy of Fine Sleuths? Quite an honor!"

"You know about the school?" asked Rollie in surprise.

"A little," said Mr. Crenshaw, as he poured tea into their cups. He passed a teacup to each of them. "My nephew attended there some years ago, and one of my dear friends is on staff there. Speaking of which . . ." He rummaged around in his briefcase and found a long white envelope, which he passed to Rollie. "Would you mind very much delivering this to my friend when you go to the Academy?"

Rollie took the envelope and read the name on it: *Professor Ichabod P. Enches*. He thought this was a very odd name, but then he had learned long ago not to judge a name since his own was unusual.

"Please help yourselves to some biscuits. I also have a little gift for your great-aunt." Mr. Crenshaw held out a small, pink box with gold ribbon. "I thought she might fancy these chocolates."

Rollie set his teacup down on the small table and took the box. "She does love chocolate. What's the occasion?"

Mr. Crenshaw shrugged his hunched shoulders. "Just a little gift from one neighbor to the other."

At that moment the secretary joined them outside. "Sir, I have the time table here. Did you wish to depart at eleven-thirty or twelve-fifteen?"

"Eleven-thirty would be best," Mr. Crenshaw told her, looking slightly annoyed by her interruption.

"Very good, sir. Will you be needing anything else?"

"No, thank you." He shooed her away with one of his gloved hands.

Clip-clop, her heels receded into the house.

Rollie stared after her as an idea formed in his brain. "That makes sense!" he suddenly exclaimed, leaping to his feet.

"What?" Cecily jolted in surprise, nearly spilling her tea.

"The class schedule! Sorry, Mr. Crenshaw, but we've got more work to do." Rollie pulled Cecily out of her chair.

"Of course, detectives!" Mr. Crenshaw waved them off. "Don't forget to deliver my letter!"

Rollie raced into his house, Cecily close at his heels. He hurried up the stairs, two at a time, gripping the banister for support. He flew into his bedroom and dropped to his knees. He picked up the closest object, the vial of dust, and read the numbers.

"One, zero, three, zero."

"Yeah, so?"

"Or you could say ten-thirty," said Rollie. "Don't you see? This is the time. Just like the train timetable that the secretary mentioned to Mr. Crenshaw. On a timetable the numbers are written just like this one with no break. But you know it's a time so you say *ten-thirty*!" He passed the vial of dust to Cecily.

Cecily's green eyes lit up. "I think you're onto something. You said class schedules had the times on them."

Rollie studied the pipe. "This class starts at eleven-thirty. See?"

"Okay, what about the key?" She passed him the key with a doubtful expression.

The numbers on the key were 0900. Rollie studied it a moment, and brightened. "Nine o'clock. The timetables put a zero first if it's a single-digit hour."

"Good. Oh, hold it, Holmes, the pen and the cap throw everything off. The pen is 1300 and—"

"And the cap is 1400." Rollie's shoulders slumped a bit. "I thought I had it."

Cecily laid out the pipe, the vial of dust, and the key on the floor in a row, and rearranged them.

"What are you doing?" Rollie wondered.

"Putting the times in order. Nine o'clock first, then ten-thirty, then eleven-thirty."

"I don't think they're times. The pen and cap don't make sense."

"Let's just say they are times and this is part of the schedule," Cecily continued. "We have a class at nine, then let's say we have morning recess. Next class, ten-thirty. Next class eleven-thirty. If they're hour-long classes, we'd get out at twelve-thirty."

"Then probably lunch," Rollie added.

"Which could be an hour. Our next class would have to be at one o'clock at least."

"Then a class at 1300 and 1400? There's no such—wait! Yes, there is! In military time, 1300 *is* one o'clock!"

"You're right!" Cecily squealed. "So 1400 would be two o'clock?"

"Yes! We've got it!" Rollie slapped a high-five with Cecily. "But we still have these letters," she reminded him.

Both of them returned to hunched postures and furrowed brows.

Cecily spoke up first, breaking the silence of concentration. "Maybe the letters are course IDs."

"They could be, but again that doesn't help us till we get to school," Rollie objected. "We're supposed to figure out the class schedule before we go."

"What else could these letters mean, then? What information are we missing?"

"Professor's name, course name, and location."

Sucking on the tip of his pencil, Rollie thought. One letter, not a few letters, so they could not be initials. What could just one letter represent? He thought of things involving one letter. A grid, a set of building directions like what his model planes came with, an address, a—

"Flats!" he shouted.

"What?"

"The letter is the address of a flat! Like 221 *b*!"

Cecily smiled. "The school *is* an apartment building!"

"I bet the flats are the classrooms," Rollie said. "So that class—whatever it is—probably is in flat H!"

"Well, done, Holmes!"

"Why, thank you." Rollie grinned and bowed dramatically.

"Now we're getting somewhere. We know the times and places."

"I still want to know what the class is and who's teaching it."

"Should we go back to our first guess?" Cecily ventured, holding up the ballpoint pen. "Writing?"

Rollie shrugged. "Could be, but what about these other items? What class would need a pipe or a key?"

"Who knows?" Cecily threw up her hands. "Remember, this school is very out of the ordinary. I wouldn't rule out any possibility."

"Let's review our class schedule, shall we?" Rollie said in his professor impersonation. Whenever he wanted to sound important, he thickened his British accent and deepened his voice to impersonate his father, whom he thought was the epitome of a professor. This always made Cecily giggle.

He cleared his throat. "Fact: young lady, at nine o'clock you have a class in room A. From there you have recess, I'm assuming. Fact: you attend a class having to do with vials of dust at ten-thirty in room D." Here he paused and held up the vial and shook it gently. "Next you must go to room F at eleven-thirty where you will learn to smoke a pipe. Not very ladylike, but I guess that won't bother you."

Cecily rolled with laughter. "Stop it! Let's write this down on paper." She scribbled down the class schedule as follows:

Key	9:00am	Room A
Recess	10:00am	?
Vial	10:30am	Room D
Pipe	11:30am	Room F
Lunch	12:30pm	?
Pen	1:00pm	Room H
Cap	2:00pm	Room G

"Looks great," Rollie commented, glancing at the schedule over her shoulder. "Do you think there's information in those words? I hadn't thought about it till you wrote them out. Key, recess, vial, pipe . . ."

"Maybe. Like a code?"

Rollie did not answer, but studied the words. He read them backwards. Key became yek. Yuck, that did not work. He inserted the room letter A into the word. He came up with akey, kaey, keay, keya . . . that was too unnerving. He rearranged the letters in key: eky, eyk, yek, yke . . . .nothing sounded remotely like a course or a professor's name.

A little light flickered through his brain.

"Initials?" he and Cecily both chimed at the same time.

"Rollie, your initials are REW. Mine are CAB. See? Mine spell a word. These words could be the initials of our teachers."

Rollie shook his head. "We don't know any of their names. We only met the headmaster and his sister."

"Once we get to school and look at the directory, we'll know right away."

"The sister!" Rollie gasped. "What was her name? Katherine something Yardsly?"

"I can't remember her middle initial, but I'm willing to bet my leftover chocolate Easter bunny that her middle initial is E," Cecily grinned.

"You still have your Easter bunny? It's July!"

Cecily shrugged. "Beside the point. We have a class with KEY: Katherine E. Yardsly."

Rollie gasped. "And we have a class with PIPE!" He held up the envelope Mr. Crenshaw had given him to deliver. "Professor Ichabod P. Enches!"

"We solved the mystery of the class schedule. I'm exhausted." Cecily fell back dramatically onto the floor, her eyes closed and her arms sprawled out.

Rollie read over the class schedule again. He had no idea what he was about to learn at Sherlock Academy, but he knew it would be thrilling. For the first time, he couldn't wait for school to start.

August the First

Having solved the class schedule, Rollie felt more confident about attending Sherlock Academy—until he realized that VIAL had four letters and clearly V did not stand for a title like *professor*. He mentioned this to Cecily the next day, and she reminded him that some people have *two* middle names or, in some rare cases, *two* last names. They decided to count this as a possibility.

Much to their surprise, the days trickled by quickly, and before they knew it, the end of July came. On Sunday, the day before August first, the Wilson household erupted into chaos in preparation for Rollie's first day of school. Lucille and Daphne pointed out they were luckier than him because their summer holiday continued until September. Edward and Stewart warned everyone they were not taking Rollie to school every day, until Mr. Wilson reminded them that Rollie would be boarding there and would be brought home every Friday evening for the weekend by the Academy's taxi service. Mrs. Wilson made sure Rollie remembered to pack his toothbrush, his slippers, his bathrobe, and "oh, what about your nice slacks, and don't forget a copy of the family portrait." Auntie Ei remained the only calm person in the manor that afternoon. She sat in the library pretending to read the newspaper, but really eavesdropping on everyone.

As Rollie passed the open library door, she spoke to him. "Rollin, come in here a moment."

Rollie hurried into the library. He almost hadn't heard her over the din of everyone else. "What is it, Auntie? Mum wants me to grab my—"

"Never mind that right now. I have something important to give you." She held out an ordinary looking jar of orange marmalade. "Take it."

Rollie took it, confused. It was a small jar holding maybe one cup of orange marmalade. It was sealed with wax, and labeled with a tag that read *A good snack for the LIBRARY*. "Uh, thanks, Auntie."

"You're very welcome, Rollin. Perhaps it will remind you of home."

"Perhaps." Rollie wanted to remind her that he didn't care for marmalade on toast and preferred only hash browns for breakfast, but he was not about to hurt the old woman's feelings by seeming ungrateful, so he nodded in agreement.

"When you've eaten it all, save the jar. You may find it useful." She folded the newspaper she had been reading, and held it out to him. "Please toss this in the rubbish. I'm through reading it."

Rollie took the *Daily Telegraph* from her and read the headline: "Scotland Yard Discovers New Lead on Herr Zilch."

"Well, this is good news, isn't it?" Rollie pointed to the headline.

"It would be if it was true," Auntie Ei said. "The Yard is always finding a new *lead* that leads nowhere in the hunt for Herr Zilch." She looked worried.

Rollie did not understand Auntie Ei's obsession with the news, in particular news on the elusive Herr Zilch. "Why are you always so interested in Herr Zilch?"

Auntie Ei frowned. "He has plagued this city for fifteen years. I have been following the news about him for that long, believe it or not. I would like nothing more than for him to be found, caught, and brought to justice for his robberies, murders, and betrayals." Her croaky voice caught slightly, and she gave a little moan.

"Are you alright, Auntie?" asked Rollie. He noticed she looked a little pale.

"It's nothing—just a bit of indigestion." She cleared her throat and continued, "Now run along and finish packing."

As Rollie left the library, she called after him, "Don't forget to pack that marmalade!"

* * * *

The next morning, being the first of August and thus the first day of school for Rollie, the Wilson family crowded together in the entry hall with Rollie's one suitcase and two boxes. Rollie endured farewell pinches and hair ruffling from his older twin brothers, and dainty hugs from his younger twin sisters. When the horse-drawn hansom pulled up to the house at eight, the family pressed together for a final farewell.

"Wash behind your ears, and air your socks and—"

"Eloise, that's enough," Mr. Wilson cut in. "Rollie's a good boy. He'll be fine."

"He's never gone away to school before."

"Mum, I'll be home on the weekends."

"Or sooner," Edward smirked. "Stew and I have a bet that you'll get homesick by Wednesday."

"I'm saying Thursday," Stewart added. "He'll be home by Thursday."

"Son, I'm saying Friday."

"Dad, I'm planning to come home every Friday."

"I know, son, I'm joking with you." Mr. Wilson gave him a wink and a firm squeeze on the shoulder. "Time to go." He picked up Rollie's suitcase and carried it to the cab. "Boys, grab his boxes!"

Grumbling, the twins each picked up a box and carried them to the cab. Lucille and Daphne helped each other carry his book bag. Mrs. Wilson pulled Rollie to her and hugged him.

"Be safe, and be good," she whispered in his ear. "Study hard and have fun."

"Bye, Mum. I'll see you in a week." Rollie turned to Auntie Ei. He leaned in for a hug, and she patted his back.

"Do you have that jar of marmalade?"

"Yes, Auntie, in one of those boxes."

"Good boy. Keep your eyes and ears open and trust your instincts." She nodded curtly and gave him a nudge down the front steps. Then she turned back inside to go read in the library.

Rollie waved to his family as he climbed inside the cab. The driver flicked the reins and started the hansom down the road to Cecily's house where she waited alone by the front gate. As the driver loaded her luggage, she climbed inside.

"Where's your family?" Rollie asked. "Didn't they want to say goodbye?"

"I said goodbye to them this morning," Cecily shrugged. "Did you have a whole farewell procession?"

Rollie ignored her question. "I can't wait to get there!" He practically bounced on his seat in anticipation.

The anticipation lasted another twenty minutes until they stopped at 221 Baker Street. The driver jumped down from his perch and opened the cab doors. "Go 'head and check in. I'll deliver yer luggage to yer rooms."

As they hopped out of the cab, Rollie and Cecily noticed the street crowded with hansoms and a long line of children leading to the front door. They found the end of the line at the corner of the building, and stepped into place.

Soon the line moved forward as the front doors opened. When Rollie and Cecily reached the front doors, they found a welcome sign that instructed them to find their first class of the day.

"This is it," Rollie exhaled. "This is when we find out if we solved the class schedule." He pulled out his notepad from his back pocket and flipped to the schedule he and Cecily had jotted down. "Room A should be on this ground floor." He led Cecily down a hallway filled with other children.

The only rooms on the first floor were the head-master's office, the library, the orientation room, and a locked storage closet. They ventured upstairs to the second floor and quickly found room A. The one-time flat had been converted into a classroom with individual desks and chairs facing a blackboard. Several charts covered the walls. The charts, all having to do with numbers and letters arranged oddly, did not make sense. Unsure if there was a seating chart, Rollie and Cecily chose two desks side-by-side, two rows from the front.

"I like to be close," Cecily whispered.

"But not too close in case we're wrong and have to leave," Rollie added, sliding into his chair.

As the clock ticked towards nine o'clock, several students filed into the classroom. They chose seats and roved their eyes around. At nine o'clock, the teacher marched into the room and towered in front of the blackboard.

"Welcome to your first class at Sherlock Academy. I am Katherine E. Yardsly."

Nine O'clock

Rollie and Cecily glanced at each other excitedly. "Students, if you are in the correct class, I will call your name from my roll sheet," Katherine E. Yardsly called, whipping out a sheet of paper from her desk. "If you are not in the correct class, you will return to the entry hall and attempt to solve the class schedule again. Understand?" She looked around the room, but did not seem to want an answer. She snapped her eyes back to the roll sheet. "Brighton!"

"Here!" Cecily answered, and blew a sigh of relief.

"Fraser!"

"Yes, that's me! I'm here!" one pale boy answered, wiping beads of sweat from his forehead.

"Hawkins!"

"Thank goodness!" one dark-haired girl exhaled.

Ms. Yardsly worked down the list, responded by relieved boys and girls. When the name Tildon was called, Rollie recognized the dark-haired boy he had met in the rearranging library. Rollie jumped when his name was called.

"Wilson!"

"Present!"

"That concludes the class list." She eyed two girls sitting in the back. "Go back downstairs to the foyer and solve the class schedule."

The two girls fumbled to their feet and ducked out the door.

"Good job to you who found your first class. Are there any questions before we commence?"

No one moved.

Ms. Yardsly turned to the blackboard, grabbed a piece of chalk, and feverishly scribbled on it. Then she spun back around, and stepped aside so the class could read the board. They were not surprised to find that it made no sense.

"Your first assignment is to learn which class this is by decoding what I have written on the board. Use your own ingenuity. You may use the paper and pencil in your desk. You have two minutes. Go!"

Rollie copied down the letters.

ADBECCDOEDFIGNHG ICJOKULRMSNE OLPEQVRESL TOUNVEW

Rollie focused on the board, his eyes widening and narrowing. He circled every third letter, like he and Cecily often did when deciphering their own codes.

He ended up with BCEI—not a word, so he tried something else. He worked backwards and got VOSVP—not a word either.

Time ticked by; a minute left.

He squinted again. He circled every other letter and found that every other letter was the alphabet: ABCDEF . . . .The remaining letters spelled . . . DECODIN—

"Time's up! Pencils down! Who has it?"

Eliot S. Tildon shot up his hand. "Decoding Course Level One!"

"You are correct. In this class, you will learn about codes and ciphers. You will learn how to crack the easiest and some of the hardest codes known. Having a resource of codes and ciphers is invaluable to a detective. You will remember that Sherlock Holmes had several occasions to crack codes. The cipher you cracked here . . ." Ms. Yardsly tapped the board with her chalk, "is one of the simpler ciphers used. You had to circle every other letter to find the message. Second assignment: use this code to write down three words to describe me. You have two minutes. Go!"

Rollie thought of three words: icy, stern, and tall. He penciled down these three words, hiding them in the alphabet. He barely finished jotting down the last letter in *tall* when she barked, "Time's up, pencils down!"

Every student dropped his pencil and stared up at her. One young girl wearing spectacles, who Rollie remembered from orientation, even put her hands up in the air to show she had dropped her pencil.

"I do a little thing called 'pair-and-share'. You pair up with a partner and share what you've learned. Wherever you have chosen to sit will be your seat the rest of the year. And whoever I assign as your partner today will be your pair-and-share partner for the rest of the term. Understand?" She did not wait for a reply. Instead she maneuvered around the room, pointing to different students, saying, "You and you, partners. You and you, partners . . ."

Rollie and Cecily were dismayed when Ms. Yardsly did not pair them up. Rollie got paired with Eliot behind him and Cecily got paired with the girl wearing spectacles, whose name was Tabbitha—Tibby for short.

"Hey, I remember you from orientation," Eliot said when Rollie turned around in his chair.

"I'm Rollin, but I go by Rollie."

"Eliot. There's no way to short-cut Eliot."

"Eli?"

Eliot made a face. "Nope, Eliot it is. How old are you?"

"I'll be twelve on November first."

71

"That's still a long ways off. You should just say eleven and a half until it's at least October."

Rollie was unsure how seriously to take Eliot, but Eliot seemed to take himself very seriously. "How old are you?"

"I just turned twelve in June."

"That's a while ago."

"Not really. It's a summer birthday and we're still in summer. See, the way I figure it, if your birthday is in the same season as you currently are, then you can say 'I'll be twelve in November.' But if your birthday is in a different season than the current one, then you should just say your age." He nodded firmly, signifying the discussion over.

"I've never heard of that before," Rollie countered. "I think everyone should be able to say what they want. There shouldn't be any rules for that sort of thing."

"If there were more rules, there'd be less crime."

"What does that have to do with birthdays?"

"Nothing. Rules do."

"I thought we were talking about birthdays."

"You changed the subject," Eliot pointed out.

"No, I didn't, you just said—"

"Rollin E. Wilson!"

Both Rollie and Eliot jumped in their seats. Ms. Yardsly towered over them, her mouth set in a firm line and her eyes locking with theirs.

"Let me clarify that pair-and-share time is to be used for assignments, not for your personal banter. Do you understand?"

This time Rollie was sure she wanted an answer. "Yes, Ms. Yardsly."

She held his gaze a moment longer, then ordered, "Swap papers, decode each other's three adjectives, and swap back." She turned on her heel and marched back to the front of the classroom.

Cecily gave Rollie a sympathetic smile, and went back to decoding Tibby's paper. Eliot held out his paper to Rollie. Rollie snatched the paper, tossed his to Eliot, and spun back around in his chair. He quickly circled every other letter and decoded Eliot's three descriptive words: *tall, loud, icy.* Funny that Eliot would use the word *icy* also. Rollie thought it was a creative adjective to use. He turned back around, swapped papers, and returned facing forward.

"Psst!" he heard behind him. "Rollie."

Rollie turned his head a bit. "I'm not talking to you. You got me in trouble."

"Sorry about that, but you should have just agreed with me. Accept my apology, chum?"

Rollie nodded reluctantly.

"Do you get what I'm saying about the birthdays?"

Rollie rolled his eyes. He could not believe Eliot brought it up again, just after they had been warned not to talk. Maybe if he ignored Eliot, then Eliot would get the hint.

"Do you? I think the season really makes a difference. And by the way, do—"

"I don't think this is important," Rollie hissed as he spun around. "So stop talking to me or we'll—"

"Rollin E. Wilson! Did I not just clarify my rules for pair-and-share? Furthermore, pair-and-share is over, so there is no excuse for your turning in your seat and talking with Eliot S. Tildon! You will write the sentence of my choosing one hundred times after class."

Rollie dropped his head on his desk partly in frustration and partly in shame. He waited for Eliot to step up and admit he had contributed to the conversation. No word came from behind. Ms. Yardsly lectured on the history of a few codes, but Rollie barely heard her. He was fuming inside. He was mad at Eliot, but also at himself. He always strove to follow the rules and apply himself as a student. His teachers always liked him and felt proud of him. Now he had made a horrible first impression to his first teacher on the first day of school. He wondered if he should mention Eliot's involvement. No, he did not want to worsen his first impression by being a tattletale.

Soon Ms. Yardsly dismissed the class and declared recess for thirty minutes on the rooftop. As the students filed out of the room, she stationed herself behind her desk.

"Rollin E. Wilson, come forth."

Rollie tiptoed up to her desk. He kept his eyes on the floor.

"Take this pencil and paper and write the sentence I dictate to you." She cleared her throat as Rollie prepared to write. "Ms. Yardsly made a hasty judgment in punishing me over Eliot."

Rollie snapped his eyes up to her.

"Rollin, I realize now Eliot got you in trouble," she said in the softest tone he had heard her use yet, though still firm. "It was noble of you to take your punishment without tattling on him. Write the sentence. Once is sufficient. It will make you feel like justice was served. That's all for today." She waved her hand at him to go.

Still surprised, Rollie stumbled back, bumping into a desk. He turned and headed for the door.

"And Rollin?"

He turned around.

"Don't make the same mistake I did by judging things too quickly."

He smiled. "Yes, Ms. Yardsly. Thank you."

The school's rooftop looked like an average recess area with tables and benches, hopscotch courts, and even a plot of grass for field games. A tall chain-link fence guarded the perimeter, and offered the students a great view of the neighborhood and nearby Regent's Park. Students sat at the tables and ate their morning snacks. Some skip-roped, played hopscotch, or stood around chatting. Rollie spotted Cecily nibbling on toast at one table. Tibby sat next to her.

"Rollie, you're back fast!" Cecily exclaimed, spewing bread crumbs everywhere. "Was it awful?"

"No, Ms. Yardsly knew it wasn't all my fault. I had to write a sentence only once."

"That's nice of her. I didn't think she could be nice."

"We misjudged her. Are you ready for our next class?" Rollie pulled out his little notepad. "Someone's class at ten-thirty in room D. That was the vial of dust."

"Right. I guess we'll know the teacher once we get there."

Rollie, Cecily, and Tibby left the rooftop and took the stairs back down to the second floor. They found room D filling up quickly. Apparently they were not the only students who liked to be early. They selected three seats in the second row. When the clock struck ten-thirty, all heads turned to the door in expectation of their teacher. They started with alarm when a woman's shrill voice exclaimed from the front of the room, "Ah-ha! Very interesting!"

A round, stout woman popped her head up and crawled out from behind the desk on all fours, a magnifying glass in one chubby hand, and a familiar vial in the other. She scrambled to her feet and puffed. "You can find the most interesting particles to study in the tiniest cracks. Remember that, children! And welcome to . . ." She trailed off, setting down the magnifying glass and vial on her desk. Her short, curly, faded red hair frizzed at the ends. She wore men's trousers and a plain white blouse. Groping in her pockets, she foraged out a piece of chalk and turned to the blackboard. "Welcome to Identification of Fingerprint, Footprint, and Ash." She wrote this on the board in curly but crooked cursive. "I am Miss Amelia S. Hertz."

Rollie and Cecily glanced at each other with the same thought. That vial did not contain dust; it contained ash, the initials of Miss Hertz's name.

"Are you in the right class?" she asked. "Hmm . . . I'll bet you'd like to know. Well, I'm not going to tell you. You must figure it out for yourself. I'm going to take a print of your right thumb. Then you have to match the print with one of those on that chart."

Everyone turned to a chart next to the door. The chart was divided into squares, each square displaying a black ink thumbprint.

"If you can match your thumbprint to one on the chart, then you're in this class. That's my class roster. I don't do well with names, but I never forget a fingerprint!" She rummaged around in her desk and found a large inkpad and a stack of white cards. She scurried around to each student and pressed his or her thumb onto the pad then onto the white card. When she came to Cecily, she sized her up with a smile. "You don't usually wear a dress, do you?"

"No, Miss Hertz. My mum made me because it's the first day of school. I usually wear my brother's trousers."

"I thought so. You didn't look comfortable. Well, there's no shame here, so you may wear those trousers if you like." Miss Hertz stopped next to Rollie and took his thumbprint.

Rollie took his white card to the chart and held it up to each print. He grew worried as he moved down the chart and did not find a match. Once he thought he had matched his, but then he looked more carefully and noticed a difference. Second to the last print, he stopped. He studied the two prints side by side. He was sure they matched. He remembered that on a class roster Wilson would come last. He smiled and resumed his seat.

"Good, everyone matched! Let's begin class."

Pipes, Pens, and Doubles

Eleven-thirty came too soon. Just as Rollie relaxed in Miss Hertz's class and started to get engrossed in fingerprint analysis, he was dismissed to his next class. Rollie felt a little stressed always hoping he had solved the class schedule correctly. So far, he and Cecily had proven their good detecting skills.

In room F, they selected similar seats as in the other two classrooms. As they sat down, they noticed their teacher sitting primly behind his desk, reading a book and smoking a pipe. He had white hair and a neat, white mustache. He looked very scholarly in his yellow tweed suit and bowtie. He cleared his throat every time he delicately turned a page. At eleven-thirty he checked the time on a gold pocket watch. He cleared his throat, closed his book, and stood. Puffing lightly on his pipe, he studied his students from beneath his bushy white eyebrows.

The students squirmed in their seats under his stare. A minute ticked by. Finally he took the pipe out of his mouth and cooed in a deep voice, "Etiquette. That's what this world needs more of. Someone tell me one good form of etiquette."

No one stirred.

"Come now, don't be bashful. Anyone?" he coaxed in a grandfatherly tone.

Slowly, Rollie raised his hand.

"Yes, lad?"

"Respecting our elders. Like calling them mister and madam."

"Very good, lad. That's positive social etiquette. Did you know that there is a level of etiquette for detectives? I am here to teach you that. This is my class entitled Spy Etiquette and Interrogation. I am Professor Ichabod P. Enches. It is good etiquette to address me as Professor Enches. I am the only faculty here with a doctorate degree, and I have taught at several universities. I am privy to the title Professor, thus I require my students to address me in that way."

Rollie raised his hand slowly again.

"Yes, lad?"

"I have a note for you, Professor." Rollie pulled Mr. Crenshaw's letter from his inner coat pocket. He got to his feet and held it out to his teacher.

Professor Enches raised his bushy eyebrows in surprise. He reached out and took the letter. "Thank you, lad." He read his name on the envelope, and stuffed it into his outer coat pocket.

"It's from Mr. Creshaw."

"Yes, thank you," Professor Enches smiled as he rested a hand on Rollie's shoulder. "It's very good of you to pass this on to me. You may resume your seat." He coughed quietly. "Now, students, I will call roll, according to good class etiquette." He picked up a roll sheet from his desk and cleared his throat. "Brighton, Cecily A."

"Present!" Cecily called, thinking that was the polite way to respond.

Professor Enches nodded approvingly. Everyone in the class responded to a name. Much to Rollie's dismay, he noticed Eliot sitting two seats behind him and made a mental note to stay clear of him.

After putting the roster away in a desk drawer, Professor Enches clasped his hands behind his back and stared at his students. Again they squirmed in their seats.

"Can anyone tell me the usual method by which Sherlock Holmes encountered a mystery?"

Rollie's ears pricked up at the mention of his hero. He shot up his hand.

"Yes, Rollin?"

"Usually a client came to his apartment and told him about the mystery."

"Very good, lad. You know your Holmes, don't you?" Enches smiled, the wrinkles creasing around his kindly eyes.

Rollie smiled back, and started to relax .

"The proper term for that activity is 'house meet,'" the professor informed, pointing at him. "Holmes always displayed a proper degree of etiquette while interviewing his clients. He also displayed etiquette while interrogating a suspect. That is what I will be teaching you in this class. Students, take notes." He turned his back on them to write on the blackboard. When he stepped away, the word *POLITENESS* stared back in capital letters.

The students looked inside their desks and found two pencils and a composition book. They took these out, and scribbled down *politeness* on the first page. For the rest of the hour, Professor Enches lectured on politeness. By the time lunch break came, the students felt like they had attended a college class.

* * * *

Although Rollie grew a little drowsy after lunch, he was eager to attend his next class at one o'clock in room H, represented by the pen. After selecting seats next to each other, Rollie and Cecily leaned their heads together to discuss the day. They had not chatted at lunch because Headmaster Yardsly had made a welcome speech to the student body.

"We're doing great so far—guessing the class schedule and all," Rollie whispered.

"I love Miss Hertz!" Cecily squealed.

"Because she wears trousers?"

"Yes, and because she told me I could wear mine."

"How did she get our fingerprints on that chart?"

Cecily shrugged. "Maybe we left prints when we were here for orientation."

"What do you think about Professor Enches?"

Cecily snored. "Boring."

"But he seems really nice," added Rollie.

Abruptly, the classroom door flew open. A man carrying an armload of long rolled papers, notebooks, a mug of pencils, and a bulging leather briefcase barged into the room. His thick, frizzy, gray hair stood up on end, as if a mighty wind had swept past him. His green trousers and coat were wrinkled, one shoelace trailed untied, and his plaid tie flapped over one shoulder. He blinked from behind super thick lenses magnifying his eyes. He resembled an owl. Sticking out his foot, the teacher tried to close the door, but leaned too much and spilled the pencils out of the mug. Tibby, who sat nearby, jumped up and gathered the pencils off the floor.

"Oh, thank you, little girl. Just put them right in this cup," he said in a high voice. Once he had all the pencils again, he tried once more to close the door with his foot. The mug tipped precariously, ready to spill.

Tibby quickly closed the door before the pencils could fall from the cup.

"Thank you again. What's your name?" He bent down and peered into her face too close for comfort.

Tibby stepped back and told him her name.

"Wonderful, wonderful." He bustled to the front of the classroom, and dropped his armload onto the desk. Not bothering to tidy the desk, he stepped closer to the students. "Welcome, boys and girls. I teach Observation Level One. You must know that it is *very*—notice how I emphasized that word—*very* important to observe *everything*. Observing is different from seeing. Holmes saw everything that everyone else saw, but he trained himself to *observe* everything and deduce information from what he noticed. You may ask, 'Mr. Notch, how can I train myself?'" Here his voice rose to imitate a child.

"Well, I'll teach you soon enough, but first we must make sure you're in the right class. I do not take roll like other classes. 'But Mr. Notch, why do you not take roll?' you may ask," he squeaked. "I am counting on you to know if you're in the right class based on my own observations. I have had plenty of time to observe each of you today. 'I did not see you anywhere, Mr. Notch'. Ah, then I am a better detective than you probably thought. Now just sit tight, and I will read some of my observations. When you are sure that I am describing you, then call out 'Here!' or 'Present!' or anything else to let me know you are that person."

Rollie and Cecily glanced at each other. Just when they thought they had met the most eccentric teacher who used the most unusual method of checking the roster, they met another one.

"Nibbles bread, talks with her mouth full, uncomfortable in dresses, left-handed, freckles on nose, auburn—"

"That's me!" Cecily beamed.

"Right you are, Miss Brighton. Welcome to my class." Mr. Notch pushed his thick glasses up his nose and continued. "Missing a coat button, ink stains on right index finger, trims his crust, hazel eyes, reddish hair . . ."

Cecily tapped a boy's shoulder in front of her.

"Me?" the boy asked with some uncertainty.

Smiling, Mr. Notch said, "Let's work on being more observant this year, Charlie B. Dover."

"I'll try, sir," Charlie mumbled.

Rollie figured that if Cecily was the first to be described, he had a while to wait until Mr. Notch got to him, since he had been at the end of all the rosters today. He guessed correctly.

"Hole in coat pocket, picks at food, short sandy-blond hair, excited brown eyes that—"

Rollie checked his coat pockets and gasped at a tiny hole in the left one. Mr. Notch kept reciting his observations until Rollie called, "Me!"

"That concludes our class roster. Welcome again, students. I have a little assignment for you all. In your desks you'll find some pencils and a composition book. Go ahead, take a peek. Those are for all your observation notes. You will take lots of notes. I want you to notice everything. Be sure to write down everything. Even little details that you think insignificant—write them down! Holmes knew the significance of details, for usually they were the key to solving the mystery. First assignment: observe someone in this room for five minutes and write down *everything*. You may begin."

Rollie swept his eyes around the room, and rested on Mr. Notch squirming behind his messy desk. Rollie jotted down a quick description of him, the desk and all the items on it. He put down his pencil, then picked it up again. When he studied the briefcase closer, he noticed *Percy E. Notch* inscribed on the briefcase.

"PEN," he mumbled to himself with a smile.

Before Rollie knew it, an hour had slipped by and he was hurrying to his last class of the day, at two o'clock in room G. He wondered how the teacher's name connected to the red ball cap.

Rollie and Cecily found room G down the hall from their other classrooms on the second floor. They dodged into the room and slipped into seats. Behind them hobbled an extremely old man on shaky knees, bowed over a cane. A patch of snowy white hair encircled his otherwise bald head. He wore a shabby sailor's pea-jacket, a frayed red scarf, stained white pants, and scuffed black shoes. He inched into the room, wheezing heavily. He took nearly three minutes to reach the front of the classroom. He turned slowly to face them, and smiled wearily. His face creased into a hundred wrinkles, but his blue eyes twinkled beneath bushy, white eyebrows.

"Good afternoon, dear ones," he croaked in a faint voice. He wheezed again, and continued. "As ye can tell, I appear to be the oldest faculty member here. But one thing ye'll learn from me is that appearances can be deceiving." He paused to catch his breath. "Ye just came from Mr. Notch's observation class, did ye not? Well then, observe me. Ye need not write anything down."

Rollie studied him closely. This teacher had to be older than his Auntie Ei; Rollie always regarded Auntie Ei as the oldest person he knew. As he moved his eyes over the old man, Rollie stopped at the teacher's hands grasping the cane. They contrasted with the rest of his appearance, for the hands bore no wrinkles, and looked not much older than his brothers' hands. How strange! Rollie stared at the old sailor, wondering if maybe . . .

"Close yer eyes, children. Tight. No peeking."

Rollie closed his eyes, his curiosity building. He listened to the sounds of rubber peeling, something sticky becoming unstuck, and the cane rattling on the floor.

"You can look, kids!" a young man's voice announced in a strong American accent.

When he opened his eyes, Rollie gaped at the young man standing before him. He had short, black hair and bright blue eyes. His face was pleasant with normal features. He was the type of man that Rollie thought he would see in any crowd anywhere. The young teacher mashed something flesh-colored and sticky in his hands.

"Like I said, appearances can be deceiving. Just a little stage makeup, fake hair, and some great acting, if I say so myself, and you have an ancient sailor before you. Want to take a guess as to which class I teach? Yes?"

"Some sort of disguise class?" Cecily piped up.

"Bingo! I teach The Art of Disguise Level One. Just between you and me, this is the most fun class in the whole school." He leaned in toward the students and whispered, "But don't tell any of the other teachers. They might get jealous and fire me."

The teacher grinned. "I'm kidding! But seriously, this is a fun class. Want to guess my name?"

"Do your initials spell out CAP?" Rollie guessed.

The young man's features grew solemn as he rushed over to Rollie. "How did you know that? Are you a spy?"

"No, sir, I—"

"Good guess, kid!" he exclaimed, patting Rollie on the back. "I surely hope you're in my class. Are you in my class?"

"I hope so, sir."

"In that case," he whispered into Rollie's ear, "my name is Chadwick A. Permiter." He jogged back to the front of the room. "Now, class, there is someone among us at this moment who knows my name." He paused dramatically and announced like a circus master, "Will that person please stand up and tell the rest of the class my name?"

Rollie shot to his feet. He already loved this teacher who had more energy than he did. "Chadwick A. Permiter!"

Mr. Permiter clapped his hands enthusiastically. "Wonderful performance, young man. If you are not in this class, I strongly encourage you to go join the London Theatre Troup. Perhaps you'll make a very convincing Macbeth. Anyways," he continued casually, waving his hand as if sweeping away that topic. "Are you ready to see through disguises and catch some bad guys? Are you ready to don a disguise and become a hero? Don't look so surprised, that's what this whole detective business is about. Are you ready?"

The students nodded and fidgeted in their seats with excitement.

"Great! First we gotta make sure you're supposed to be here. I'm gonna do this in a quick, painless way—like ripping off a band-aid. Is there anyone here named Herbie Z. Frecklebottom?" He searched earnestly around the room.

The children stifled giggles.

"No? Well, that's the only student who is not supposed to be here. I know that everyone else is in the right place." He spun around to the blackboard, but then spun back around. "By the way, if anyone does run into Herbie Z. Frecklebottom, please tell him the principal—I mean, *headmaster*— wants to see him."

At the second mention of this ridiculous name, all the students openly giggled.

Mr. Permiter put his hands on his hips. "How dare you laugh at poor Herbie Frecklebottom! He comes from the prestigious Frecklebottom and Wartnose families!"

The children roared with laughter. For a moment Mr. Permiter held his serious composure, but then burst out laughing with them. "There are no such people—at least not here. I can't speak for the rest of the world." Mr. Permiter hopped onto his desk and sat cross-legged atop it. "Let's discuss my disguise. Did anyone see through it? Be honest. Don't sound smart just to impress me. It *will* work." He winked at them. "Yes, Rollie?"

Rollie widened his eyes in surprise at the mention of his name.

"Yes, I know your names already. Put your hand down, Rollie."

Rollie smiled. "I noticed your hands. They didn't look old."

Mr. Permiter snapped his fingers. "A dead give-away. Good one, Rollie!"

"Thank you, Mr. Permiter."

"You can call me Mr. Chad. But not you." He pointed to a girl right in front of him. When she looked crestfallen, he grinned. "Kidding! You may all call me Mr. Chad."

"Mr. Chad? I noticed something else."

"Let's have it, Rollie."

"That old sailor disguise was the same one that Sherlock Holmes wore in *The Sign of the Four*."

"Bingo! A true Sherlockian! If I didn't know any better, I'd say you were a detective. Now to tell you a little bit about myself," Mr. Chad began, as if someone had just asked him about his life. "I'm American, grew up in New York City, and yes, it is a grand city, and yes, I am personal friends with Lady Liberty. Last year, I came here to teach. I'm still the new kid on the block, so to speak. I love the Brits, but hate your food. It's very boring. And I refuse to wear a tie." He pointed to his collar. "Professor Enches always gives me a hard time and tells me it's professional etiquette to wear a tie." He shrugged. "One last thing I will tell you: this school is full of mysteries, so keep a wary eye out!"

* * * *

"I think Mr. Chad is my favorite teacher," Rollie said as he and Cecily skipped downstairs.

"He's very funny. I like his accent, but Miss Hertz is my favorite."

They reached the downstairs hall where a line had formed. The students waited turns to read the dormitory assignment on the wall. Some moans of disappointment and some squeals of excitement could be heard as students read with whom they would room.

"I'm going to love being here!" Cecily exclaimed.

"Me too! Especially since Mr. Chad said there are plenty of mysteries here." Rollie stepped up to the list tacked on the wall. He found his name. "I'm in room O on the fourth floor. I'm rooming with . . . Oh no! Eliot! And some other boy named Rupert."

"You don't like Eliot?"

"He's annoying. Where are you?"

Cecily used her finger to track down her name. "I'm on the third floor in room J. I'm with Tibby and Margot."

They scooted out of the way and mounted the stairs. Cecily waved goodbye on the third floor, and Rollie continued on up to the fourth. On the fourth floor, the hallway bustled with boys. Two tall boys tossed a yellow ball to each other, another three boys chased each other in and out of open rooms, and more boys bumped past each other trying to find their rooms. Rollie found his at the end of the hallway. When he stepped inside, he spotted Eliot leaning out the one window. The room was small with three beds lined against three of the walls. One desk stood under the window. Rollie found his suitcase, boxes, and book bag stacked on the bed nearest the door. He strode over and opened the suitcase.

Eliot turned. "Hello, roomie."

"Hello," Rollie mumbled.

"Glad to be rooming with you. I was nervous I'd be rooming with someone I didn't know."

"Have you met Rupert yet?"

Eliot shrugged. "He hasn't been up yet. It's great that we have classes together, too. Although I shouldn't be surprised, since all first year students take the same classes together."

Rollie draped his bathrobe over the end of his bed. "Do you know anything about our extra classes? For math and science and all that?"

"You didn't hear? That's what they call Independent Studies—IS for short." Eliot opened the deep bottom desk drawer. "All your textbooks are in here. We follow a syllabus. We have to do it in our own time. I'm thinking if I get up early I can do a few subjects before breakfast. That way I'll have more free time in the afternoon. Plus I want to use the desk first. I hope you don't mind. I set my alarm for five o'clock."

Rollie groaned. "Five o'clock! That's so early. Why don't you study in the library?"

"It's all the way downstairs," Eliot protested. "I'll be really quiet. Actually, you should wake up and study with me."

"No, thanks. I work better in the afternoon."

"You should get it done in the morning."

"Don't tell me what to do," Rollie snapped. His head swam with the events of the day. He needed a little peace to settle his thoughts.

Eliot held up his palms in a gesture of defense. "Cranky! I'm just trying to be a good chum."

"Sorry, Eliot. My head is so full right now."

"I know what you mean. You know what I do to relax? I read my comic books."

"Who do you read?"

"Sherlock Holmes."

"Sherlock Holmes comic books?"

"My grandpa gave them to me. They're really rare." Eliot tossed his pillow aside and grabbed a small stack of black and white comic books. "You can borrow them whenever you want. Start with this one." He held up one titled *The Adventure of the Speckled Band.*

"I love that mystery! Thanks, Eliot." Rollie took the comic book and lay down on his bed.

Maybe Eliot would not be such a bad roommate after all.

Rollie the Postman

By Friday, Rollie had grown accustomed to his new school. He memorized his schedule, regained his appetite, and slept through the night. Surprisingly, Eliot studied quietly in the wee hours of the morning, and used a flashlight to read by. Rupert kept to himself, being a boy with a solemn face; he never appeared happy to be there.

But Rollie was.

He liked having different teachers for different subjects. He liked that the teachers never gave homework. He liked that most of class time was used for practicing lessons, instead of listening to lectures—except for Professor Enches, who enjoyed lecturing in a boring manner. Rollie deemed Mr. Chad his favorite. Mr. Chad often called on Rollie to answer questions, or used Rollie to demonstrate applying a false nose or eyebrows. Rollie found him interesting, and loved listening to his American accent. Rollie had never been this excited about school.

Late Friday morning, Rollie sat listening to Professor Enches ramble on about the polite manner to introduce oneself to a potential client seeking help with a mystery. At first Rollie took notes diligently, but after thirty minutes his mind wandered. He thought about his family and what it would be like returning home for the weekend later that afternoon. He hoped his brothers would not tease him too much, but he did hope his family asked lots of questions about his week. He hoped the dinner conversation centered on him—he did not hope too high, though.

"Always make direct eye contact. This is not only polite, but also assertive, and it shows your client that you are interested, attentive, and courageous enough to hear whatever frightful tale they are about to disclose to you."

Rollie heard Professor Enches in the background, so started with surprise when he felt the professor brush past him. An envelope landed on his desk with a light slap. Professor Enches continued walking down the rows of desks, and did not bother to look back. Rollie read the front: *To Mr. Crenshaw.*

Did Professor Enches mean for Rollie to deliver this? Why did Rollie have to be their postman?

As soon as class was dismissed, Rollie leaped to his feet and dodged around his classmates to Professor Enches's desk, where the professor sorted through his notes. When Enches spotted Rollie heading for him, he gave the boy a kindly smile.

"Professor, sir, did you want me to deliver this for you?"

"Yes, of course—if you don't mind, that is," Enches said.

"I don't mind," Rollie said hesitantly. "I just wondered why me instead of the post."

"I suppose I can let you in on our little secret." Enches leaned on his desk and beckoned Rollie to step closer. In a low voice he told him, "Mr. Crenshaw and I are planning a special party for the staff here, and have been discussing details through our letters. But we can't use the post because all incoming and outgoing mail at the Academy is inspected as a precaution against enemies."

Rollie's brown eyes widened. "I didn't know the Academy had enemies."

Enches' face grew grave. "Oh, yes, but that is a different conversation." He cleared his throat. "Since you live next door to Mr. Crenshaw and you see me on a daily basis, we thought you'd be our perfect ally to deliver our correspondences. You're sure you don't mind?"

"No, sir, I don't mind."

Professor Enches patted him on the shoulder. "Good lad."

* * * *

"Rollie, tell us all about your first week of school!" his mother exclaimed at the dinner table later that evening.

"Solve any big cases yet?" Edward snickered through a mouthful of potatoes.

"Rooming with any villains?" Stewart added.

"Boys," Mrs. Wilson warned. "Let Rollie speak."

"It's great, Mum, I really love it!"

"Whoa!" Stewart commented. "The kid's eyes just got really wide when he said that!"

"He must be pretty excited!" Edward gasped dramatically.

"What are your classes like?" Mr. Wilson spoke up, regarding Rollie over his spectacles.

"I have five classes every day. It's sorta like college, Dad. One of my teachers is actually a professor."

"Who is he? Maybe I know him."

"Professor Ichabod P. Enches."

"Ichabod? Very odd name."

"His initials spell PIPE."

Mr. Wilson chewed thoughtfully on his roasted chicken. "PIPE! Wasn't that one of the items in your hollow book?"

"Yeah! Dad, it's so clever. All those items were the initials of all my teachers, and—"

"That *is* clever!" Stewart exclaimed.

"What item am I?" Edward asked. "What's an EPW?"

"Nothing. But I'm a SAW. Ha!" Stewart socked his twin in the shoulder.

"Fact: I don't know any Enches," Mr. Wilson continued. "Never heard of an Enches. Where did he get his degree?"

Rollie shrugged. "He didn't say. Oh! One of my teachers is American. He's from New York City."

"Lucky bloke!" Edward exclaimed. "Someday I'm going to New York City."

"You'll never go. It's too expensive," Stewart said matter-of-factly.

"I want to see the Statue of Liberty!" Lucille piped up.

"Lady Liberty," Daphne chimed in.

After dinner, the family went their separate ways. Rollie headed upstairs, anxious to be in his room again. As he passed Auntie Ei's bedroom, he heard a distinct clearing of the throat, so he poked his head in her doorway. The old woman sat in her comfy armchair next to a glowing fireplace; she was reading the *Daily Telegraph*, and nibbling on the chocolates from Mr. Crenshaw. Rollie stifled a smile when he realized that the box was almost empty. He knew exactly what he was going to give Auntie Ei for Christmas now.

"Did you want something, Auntie Ei?"

"You were not able to tell us much at the dinner table tonight." She kept her eyes on her newspaper.

"That's okay. I'm used to it."

"Is it a fine school? Are you studying hard?" Her eyes did not look up as she turned a page and folded the newspaper.

"Yes, Auntie. I really love it." Rollie ventured into the bedroom. He had set foot in that room only two other times before: once to collect some ashes from her fireplace to study under his magnifying glass, and another time to read to her when she fell ill. The first time he got scolded, and the second time he got thanked. He wondered what he would get this time. "One teacher said the school was full of mysteries. That got me excited."

Her eyes snapped up. "Mysteries? What kinds of mysteries?"

"I don't know yet, Auntie."

"Well, keep a wary eye all the same." Her eyes dropped back down to the *Daily Telegraph*.

"That's what Mr. Chad told me."

"The American teacher?"

"Yeah, he's really fun."

"He is relatively new on staff at the Academy. I do not know much about him. On the contrary, you can fully trust Headmaster Yardsly," added Auntie Ei. "I've known him for years and I cannot think of anyone more trustworthy."

"Really?" Rollie eyed her as curiosity tickled his brain. "How do you know him—"

"Did you like the marmalade?" interrupted Auntie Ei.

Rollie had forgotten about his great-aunt's odd gift. "I haven't eaten any yet," he confessed in a small voice.

"Well, you should enjoy it soon before it goes bad."

"I'll try some this week."

"It's of no consequence." To herself she mumbled, "At this point, anyway."

Rollie caught that last statement. He watched his old great-aunt sitting cozily by the fire, newspaper in hand. For the first time, Rollie grew suspicious of his great-aunt. Suspicious she knew more than she let on. Suspicious she had a connection to his new school. And suspicious she had a different purpose for giving him the jar of marmalade.

Auntie Ei took a bite of chocolate, groaned, and dropped the half-eaten piece back in the pink box.

"Still indigestion?" asked Rollie.

Auntie Ei rolled her eyes. "I do not have many sins, but my love of chocolate is one of them. I am afraid at my age sugar does me no favors. I will be fine." She closed the pink box.

"Are you finished reading? Would you like me to toss the paper for you?" Rollie offered.

Auntie Ei looked up at him, her gray eyes soft. "Thank you, Rollin, yes. I fear if I read much more I will have a heart attack." She passed the newspaper to him with a sigh and picked up a book off of her end table.

Rollie scanned the newspaper and knew why the headline troubled Auntie Ei so much. It heralded yet another crime by Herr Zilch. Rollie wanted to ask his great-aunt more about the criminal mastermind, but he could tell she was not in the mood to discuss any more. She opened her book and did not acknowledge him further.

* * * *

Rollie pushed the doorbell. He fingered the envelope in his left hand. From inside he heard the *clip-clop, clip-clop* of heels upon marble floors. The door opened.

"Good afternoon," the young, brassy-haired secretary greeted in a pleasant voice with a pleasant expression. "May I help you?"

Rollie answered, "I have a letter for Mr. Crenshaw." He held it out to her.

"Would you like to deliver it yourself?" she asked in a musical tone.

"Sure."

"Follow me."

Clip-clop, clip-clop. Rollie followed her through the house—a very grand house with high ceilings decorated with Italian frescos. He passed a library with barren shelves and covered furniture. The parlor also looked unoccupied with white sheets covering sofas and armchairs, and the fireplace was cold and dark. A magnificent crystal chandelier, veiled with cobwebs, hung above a grand marble staircase. As he passed the staircase, Rollie glanced up at the landing and spotted large oil portraits of stern military leaders guarding the wall. The mansion felt cold and empty. Rollie thought it a little strange that Mr. Crenshaw had still not fully moved into the mansion even though he had been living there since last winter. He wondered if maybe the elderly man had difficulty unpacking his things, for he moved around stiffly and slowly.

The secretary led Rollie through the sparse kitchen to the back garden. Mr. Crenshaw sat in his usual spot under the willow tree. He struggled to his feet as Rollie stepped outside.

"Good afternoon, young neighbor. How are you today?" He extended one of his gloved hands.

"Fine, thank you." Rollie shook it and held out the envelope to him.

Mr. Crenshaw took it with a nod. "I am much obliged. I hope you do not mind being our little postman. Did Ichabod tell you about our little secret we're planning?"

"Yeah, he told me all about it."

"Good. Tell me, how are you enjoying Sherlock Academy?"

"I love it."

"Is Sullivan Yardsly still headmaster?"

"Yeah, he is."

"How many students attend?"

"Not sure. I'd say about eighty. The dorm list had about that many names on it."

"That's a good number. How many faculty?"

"There are six including the headmaster."

"Have you solved the Rearranging Library yet?" Mr. Crenshaw asked.

Rollie shook his head. "Not yet."

Mr. Crenshaw smiled, the creases around his sunken eyes deepening. "Well, you're a clever detective. I am sure it's only a matter of time before you do."

"Thank you. I better be going, sir."

"Of course, young man. Thank you again for your service. And remember, mum's the word." He winked.

As Rollie started to leave, Mr. Crenshaw stopped him.

"How did your aunt like the chocolates I sent over?" he asked.

Rollie grimaced. "They gave her a stomachache."

"Oh, I'm sorry to hear that, and a little embarrassed. I did have another box to give her, but . . ." he gestured to a small blue box with a silver ribbon on the tea table. He frowned and drummed his fingers on the head of his cane.

"Ah, wait just a moment," he said smiling as he shuffled over to a corner of the garden. He returned with a pair of shears and clipped several snapdragons and purple hyacinth blossoms from the garden. He pulled out a plain white handkerchief and wrapped the bouquet before handing it to Rollie.

"Perhaps these would suit her better."

"Well, she did eat the chocolates rather quickly." said Rollie.

"In that case, why don't you wait a day or two before giving her this other box." He handed it to

Rollie as well. "These aren't quite as rich and shouldn't bother her."

Rollie took the box of chocolates, said thank you, and bid his elderly neighbor farewell.

The Silent Library

"You don't even like marmalade. Why did Auntie Ei give you a jar of it?" asked Cecily.

Rollie and Cecily sat side by side in the horse-drawn cab. It was a foggy Monday morning, typical of England, but disappointing to summer vacationers. The hansom bounced along towards London. Rollie had just told Cecily about Auntie Ei's odd gift.

"She won't just come out and tell me, but I know there's some reason," said Rollie. "This weekend, she asked me if I liked it, and I said I hadn't tried it yet. She seemed disappointed that I hadn't."

"Well, your great-aunt is a mysterious soul," muttered Cecily.

"Mysterious? You think so?"

Cecily laughed. "Odd for sure."

"I have to agree with that."

Within fifteen minutes, the cab pulled up to 221 Baker Street. Rollie and Cecily both looked around in confusion as they stepped out. The front steps of the school were bustling with people. A squad of blue uniformed policemen patrolled the front doors to keep nosy on-lookers from entering the building. A few other students who had just arrived stood on the curb unsure what to do.

"What happened?" Cecily asked.

Rollie led her to a nearby policeman guarding the front door. "Excuse me, sir, may we enter?"

The man glared down at him. "Are you a student?"

"Yes, sir, we all are," Rollie answered, indicating Cecily and the three other students behind him.

"Very well, go ahead." The policeman nodded toward the front doors, and called into the building, "Inspector Pembly! Students entering!"

The entry hall was no quieter than outside. Several plainclothes inspectors—Rollie guessed from Scotland Yard—stood around interviewing staff and writing notes.

"Do you have night security?" Inspector Pembly, with a fedora pushed back on his head, asked the headmaster.

"No, there's never been a need," Headmaster Yardsly replied, shaking his head sadly. Noticing the new arrivals, he turned and told them, "First hour classes are postponed. There's an assembly on the roof in ten minutes." He turned back to Pembly.

"What do you think happened here?" Cecily whispered.

Rollie went on tiptoes, trying to see past the inspector and the headmaster. Beyond them a few more policemen lingered around the library. "I think we're about to find out. Let's head to the roof." He led the others upstairs.

Along their way up the four flights of stairs, they bumped into a few policemen. Some asked students a few questions, some measured the halls, and some photographed the windows. On the roof, the children found the student body and faculty sitting at picnic tables. A podium stood before them. Rollie and Cecily found seats next to Tibby and Eliot.

"Pretty exciting, huh?" Eliot poked Rollie in the ribs.

"I guess. What happened?"

"A mystery! And we've got to solve it!"

"*We* do?"

"Sure. Between you and me, I think this is all a set up to give us some field experience."

"It's a pretty elaborate set up," Rollie muttered doubtfully.

"Want to be my partner?"

"You're getting ahead of yourself. We better wait to hear from Headmaster Yardsly before we pick partners."

"Hey," Cecily cut in. "I'm always Rollie's partner."

"Tibby, want to be partners?" Eliot asked, leaning over Rollie to speak with her.

Tibby glanced at him nervously. She started to say something, but Headmaster Yardsly appeared behind his podium.

"SLEUTHS!" his voice boomed, demanding everyone's attention. Back to a normal pitch, he continued, "A burglary has been committed here at Sherlock Academy. An *attempted* burglary, that is. This is not a mock crime for fieldwork, this is the real deal, if you will." He paused and took a sip of water.

The students whispered their speculations to each other.

"AHEM!" Headmaster Yardsly yelled more as a word than an actual clearing of his throat. "All you need to know is that the library was broken into last night, but nothing was taken. We will have a few policemen patrolling the grounds today. You are dismissed to your regular classes!"

The students scrambled to their feet and filed downstairs where they dispersed to their classrooms. Since it was only nine-fifteen, Rollie, Cecily, Eliot, and Tibby headed to Ms. Yardsly's class. There Ms. Yardsly posted herself behind her desk. Her hands rested on two tall stacks of books. An unusual amount of chatter filled the classroom as the students took their seats.

"Quiet, students, quiet!" Ms. Yardsly ordered, eyeing them with her cold stare. "I do not want to hear another word about the burglary. We are here to learn codes and ciphers. I have your textbooks. I need two volunteers."

Whenever Ms. Yardsly asked for volunteers, nobody raised a hand. Everyone felt nervous about helping, afraid they might do the wrong thing under her watchful eyes. Ms. Yardsly commissioned her own volunteers.

"Rollin E. Wilson! Eliot S. Tildon! Quickly, quickly, don't dawdle!"

The two boys bustled up to her desk.

"Take a stack of textbooks and distribute them to your classmates." She turned to the blackboard and feverishly scribbled a code on it. She always wrote with such fervor that she often broke her chalk.

Rollie and Eliot struggled to grip the tall stack of heavy textbooks. They held the books in their arms, and steadied the stacks under their chins. They moved around the classroom, squatting a bit so each student could take a book. They kept the last books for themselves and returned to their desks without incident.

Whew! Rollie breathed, glad nothing embarrassing had happened, and glad Ms. Yardsly had kept her eyes on the board and not on him.

Ms. Yardsly spun around. "Cecily A. Brighton! Please read the title of our textbook aloud."

Cecily licked her lips. "*On Secret Writings: One Hundred Sixty Separate Ciphers.*" She gasped, and added, "Sherlock Holmes wrote this!"

"You are correct. It is one of his many monographs. Turn to page seven."

The flipping of pages could be heard.

Rollie felt a little overwhelmed as he thumbed through the 325-page textbook filled with jumbles of letters and numbers. He closed his eyes. All he wanted to think about was the burglary. It had shaken him up to think the school was not entirely safe, but it had also heightened his detective senses. He liked having a real mystery to solve. He hoped to do a little investigation of his own, which got him thinking . . .

Why would someone attempt a burglary, but not steal anything? Maybe the thief had been interrupted and fled the scene before taking anything. Now that he thought about it, what was the thief after in the library? Nothing but books there, which were difficult to track down since all the shelves rearranged themselves every twenty-four hours. Hmm . . . why *did* the shelves rearrange every twelve hours? Ms. Yardsly had never explained that at orientation. Maybe there was something valuable in the library after all . . .

Finally, Ms. Yardsly dismissed them to recess. Rollie thought of joining a group of boys playing rugby, but decided to visit the library instead. Cecily noticed him start downstairs, and caught up to him.

"Are you going to investigate the library?" she asked.

"I just want to take a quick look around," said Rollie.

They wove their way downstairs against the flow of upward traffic. When they reached the first floor, they found it empty and wondered where the policemen had gone. They entered the library.

The light was off, so the room was very dim. A board against the window blocked weak sunlight. Cecily pointed out that the pane had been broken, and Rollie figured the thief must have entered through the window from the outside. He padded across the room to the lamp on the side table. He pulled its chain to turn it on. The soft glow melted away any spookiness they both felt. They studied the walls of tall bookcases, and Rollie swept his eyes along one shelf at his eye-level. The titles varied, stacked in no particular order.

The Complete Poems of Edgar Allan Poe.

The History of the Airplane and Other Flying Machines.

Art History: Renaissance.

"I wonder where my Sherlock Holmes book is," Rollie said quietly

"Who knows?" replied Cecily with a shrug. "These shelves mixed everything up."

Rollie counted the bookcases lining the walls and towering up to the ceiling; there were eight. He remembered watching the books slide and drop and raise and move around. He felt a little hopeless as he perused the hundreds of books, and imagined them shuffling around soon.

"Do you think any of the other students have found their books yet?" asked Rollie. "Like the third or fourth years?"

"We should ask some of them," said Cecily as she studied the stacks of books on one shelf.

"They probably submitted Sherlock Holmes books like us," guessed Rollie. "Which means there should be quite a few Holmes books on the shelves."

He stepped up to a center bookcase and ran his finger and eyes down each stack of books. He reached the bottom shelf when he faintly heard the bell from the rooftop signaling recess over.

"Time for Miss Hertz's class." Cecily headed for the door.

"Almost done," muttered Rollie.

He quickly checked the last books on the bottom shelf, flicked off the lamp, then bounded upstairs with Cecily. He puzzled over what he had found, or rather what he had *not* found: any Sherlock Holmes books.

Eighty Missing Holmes

"I apologize for being a few minutes delayed," Professor Enches announced as he hurried into the classroom. His long legs took him to the front in barely six strides. "The disturbing events of last night had me detained. I will say no more. Tardiness is a form of poor etiquette. However, if it is due to imperative detective work, it is somewhat justified. If you are ever tardy due to a case, be sure to express that to your client, and apologize sincerely. Proceed to present the fruit of your tardiness, so they can see its justification. Understand?"

The students had learned it was unnecessary to answer his questions, which were frequently rhetorical. Expecting no answer, Professor Enches found his pipe in his pocket, scratched a match on his matchbook, and lit the pipe. After a few puffs, he nodded in satisfaction, then stared at his students for a few moments: a ritual he practiced every class period.

Remembering Mr. Crenshaw's second letter in his pocket, Rollie raised his hand.

Professor Enches puffed on his pipe and nodded at Rollie, indicating permission to speak.

"I have another letter for you."

Professor Enches coughed, took two strides over to Rollie, and took the letter from his outstretched hand. "Thank you, lad. Please see me after class." He stuffed the envelope into his outer coat pocket and returned to the front. "Students, today we will discuss correct etiquette when interviewing a client of the opposite gender. If you are a male, then a client of the opposite gender would be a female, and vice versa. Now let's suppose that a client enters your office and . . ."

Please see me after class . . .

Those words pounded in Rollie's ears. Was he in trouble? For delivering Mr. Crenshaw's letters? Surely not! Rollie wished Professor Enches' lecture would hurry by, but of course it did not. Rollie found that whenever he anticipated something time slowed, making the wait unbearable. Yet whenever he reached that anticipated moment time sped up, ending the excitement too soon.

Class ended, students headed to lunch, and Rollie waited for Professor Enches. Cecily raised her eyebrows at Rollie, wondering what could be the matter this time. She ducked out the door. The professor stepped up to Rollie.

"Lad, I thank you for delivering Mr. Crenshaw's and my correspondences. It's very good of you." Enches gave a little nod. "However, it is poor etiquette to interrupt class to deliver those letters to me in front of your peers. Besides, we don't want to give the surprise party away, right?"

Rollie nodded. "Right, sir."

"Of course not. Would you drop the letters on my desk before class commences?"

"Yes, sir, if that's what you'd like."

Professor Enches puffed and nodded. "Good lad. Dismissed."

* * * *

Students filled the tables on the roof to eat their lunches and chat with their friends. Most conversations revolved around the attempted burglary. Rollie smiled gratefully at Cecily as he slid into a seat she had saved for him.

"In trouble again? That's not like you," Cecily commented between bites of her sandwich.

Rollie leaned in and whispered. "It was about Mr. Crenshaw's letters. It was nothing." He unwrapped his sandwich and unscrewed his milk bottle cap.

Wesley Livingston, the fourth-year rugby and fencing team captain, slid onto the bench across from Rollie. He flashed a smile of perfect teeth. "Rollie, right? You should join our rugby game after lunch."

Rollie grinned. "Thanks, but I've got some work to do." He took a sip of milk. "Could you help me by answering a few questions?"

Wesley laughed. "Sure, detective."

"Did you bring a Sherlock Holmes book as your favorite book for orientation?"

Wesley nodded as he chewed his sandwich.

Rollie continued, "And you put your book in the Rearranging Library?"

More nodding and chewing from Wesley.

"Have you found your book yet?"

Wesley shook his head. "You'd think after nearly four years I'd have cracked that library."

"Have *you*?" Eliot piped up, turning to Rollie.

"No, but I want to."

Eliot looked relieved.

"How many students are enrolled here?" Rollie asked.

Wesley said, "There are eighty—twenty per grade every year."

Rollie chewed thoughtfully. "Do you know any students who *didn't* bring a Sherlock Holmes book?"

Wesley took a swig of milk. "Now that I think about it, no."

"Interesting."

Cecily giggled. "Rollie, there's nothing interesting about *that*. It's no surprise that students would bring a Sherlock Holmes book to *Sherlock* Academy. Even if they didn't read much Holmes, any smart student would bring one anyway. Everyone wants to fit in."

Cecily was right about that. What Rollie found interesting was that there could be eighty Sherlock Holmes books in the library. He jumped to his feet, stuffing the last of his sandwich into his mouth and draining the last of his milk.

"Where are you going?" Cecily questioned.

"I've got some work to catch up on."

Eliot pointed an accusing finger at him. "I *told* you that you should get your work done in the mornings. It's the best time."

Rollie rolled his brown eyes. "See you later. Thanks, Wesley."

"Sure thing, detective!" Wesley called.

"Wait up!" Cecily chased after him.

They darted across the roof before anyone else could follow them, and skipped down four floors to the library. As they paused in the doorway to catch their breath, they spotted Mr. Notch bumbling down the hall toward them. His arms grappled with his briefcase, papers, and mug of pencils as usual.

"Hello, Mr. Notch," Rollie and Cecily chimed in unison.

Mr. Notch stumbled to a halt, not seeing his students until he nearly bumped into them. "Oh, hello, hello. Rollin, is it? Cecily, eh? Thank goodness I remembered. I try so hard to remember names. How are you today?"

"Fine, thank you," Cecily answered.

"Just thought we'd take a try at the Rearranging Library," said Rollie.

"Did you now? Good, good. Would you like a hint?"

Rollie's eyes brightened. "We sure would!"

"Of course you would. Who wouldn't want a hint? Keep one thing in mind: things are not what they seem on the outside." He attempted to tap his nose to gesture smartness, but found he had no free hands. He almost dropped his pencil mug in the attempt. "Oh! Never mind, I'm sure you get the idea. I'm off to class."

"What time is it?" Rollie asked with a hint of panic.

"Don't worry. You still have twenty minutes. I try to get to class early so I don't have to come in juggling all this." He smiled, blinked behind his ultra-thick glasses, and staggered down the hall toward the staircase.

Rollie and Cecily stepped into the library and pulled the lamp chain. They decided to work from each end of the room and meet in the middle. Rollie hurried to the far left bookcase. He had to stand on his tiptoes to see the top shelves. As he worked down the books, he got quicker at reading the titles. Within a few minutes, he reached the bottom shelf and finished checking that bookcase. He moved on to the second bookcase. Racing his eyes and fingers, he finished checking four bookcases before the bell rang. He met Cecily in the middle, and plopped down on the floor between two shelves.

"Well?" he asked her as he rested his head against the wall.

Cecily sat cross-legged on the floor next to him. "No Sherlock Holmes books. So weird! Even if no one else submitted a Holmes book there should at least be two—mine and yours!"

Rollie sighed. A mystery burrowed in his mind: there were no Sherlock Holmes books on any of the eight bookcases. Where were all the students' books? The students had placed their books on shelves, watched them get shuffled around, and lost sight of them. Obviously, they had lost sight of them because—

"They disappeared." Rollie shook his head in bewilderment.

"How could eighty books disappear?" wondered Cecily.

"Did someone take them?" Rollie said.

"What for? And what—" Cecily stopped mid-sentence.

"Huh?" Rollie followed her gaze up to the side of the bookcase he was leaning against. "Is that a hole?"

Rollie and Cecily scrambled to their feet. Rollie peered into a hole in the side of the bookcase on his left. It was not too deep or too large a hole. Gingerly, he stuck his hand in the hole, feeling the width and height and depth. He felt a raised shape sticking out from the backing. He traced it with his fingers. It felt like the number eight. He retrieved his hand and studied the side of the opposite bookcase on his right. Another similar hole. He fingered the inside—a seven, he guessed.

"What are these holes for?" Cecily stuck her hand into one of them.

Rollie did not answer her, for his brain was steaming ahead with an idea. The holes were a little bigger than an empty toilet paper roll. Smaller than a paint can. More like the size of . . .

"A jar!" he exclaimed.

Cecily whirled around to face him. "What are you talking about?"

"These holes are about the size of a jar, right?" he replied.

Cecily looked confused. "I guess."

Ring! Ring!

Lunch recess ended. Rollie groaned, but stuck his hand in one more hole in another bookcase—a six. Bouncing with excitement, he sprinted out the library, forgetting to turn off the lamp. He took the stairs two at a time, Cecily at his heels. Panting, they rushed into class and took their seats. Rollie glanced at Mr. Notch's desk: no teacher, no briefcase or papers, and no pencil mug.

At that moment, Mr. Notch burst into the room, his arms still full of everything he had carried earlier. As he passed Rollie, he grinned sheepishly.

"There's always something!"

A Jarring Clue

Although Rollie enjoyed Mr. Notch's class, he had come to look forward to Mr. Chad's class more, which promised interesting disguises and funny anecdotes. Today's class did not disappoint.

"So what gave me away this time?" Mr. Chad grinned at his students as he scratched his neck beneath a red cravat. "Cecily!"

"You're wearing your Converse sneakers. I don't think a common loafer would wear Converse sneakers."

"Bingo! Like hands, shoes can be dead giveaways, too. Now, this woman I knew who worked in a New York department store told me that shoes can either make or break an outfit. Does anyone know what that means? Tibby!"

"My older sister says that, too. It means shoes can make an outfit look good or bad."

"Bright as a penny! Or pence, I guess. While that is true, not too many people notice a person's shoes.

But you're all bright detectives, so there was no fooling you!" He wiggled out of a seedy coat with the collar turned up. Next he whipped off his cap and cravat. He tossed the whole disguise into a costume box he kept in the corner, and sat cross-legged atop his desk. "Let's review: nose-hairs and earlobes can give a disguise away, right?"

The students giggled and shook their heads.

"No? What can give disguises away? Hands and . . . ?"

"Shoes!" everyone chimed.

"I'm so proud!" Mr. Chad gushed, wiping away imaginary tears from his twinkling blue eyes. "By the way, the fun thing about a disguise like that one—" He pointed to the ragged coat, red cravat, and frayed cap in the corner, "—is that you can be any type of worker or loafer. Maybe you're looking for work as a carpet layer, a plumber, a napkin-stasher. . . . Oh, there is such a job. Extra points if you can identify that loafer disguise!"

Hands flashed up.

"Tildster?"

Eliot grinned, "Holmes wore it in *The Adventure of the Blue Carbuncle*."

"I can't teach you smarties anything more today. Class dismissed!"

Mr. Chad always stood at the door to shake the students' hands and say a positive word or two to them as they left. Rollie usually tried to be last so he could linger with his favorite teacher, but not today. Today he was anxious to go to his room and search for something in particular. He hastily shook Mr. Chad's hand, and tried to squeeze away.

"Whoa there, horsey!" Mr. Chad tightened his grip on Rollie's hand. "Where are you off to in such a hurry?"

"Sorry, Mr. Chad, I've got a lot of work to do."

Mr. Chad studied Rollie's face. He leaned down and said in a low tone, "You're onto a mystery, aren't ya? I can see that spark in your eyes. Well, keep up the good work, Rollie. I could tell from the first day of class that you'd make a great detective."

Rollie's face flushed with pleasure. He soaked up any compliment he could get, especially from someone he admired like his favorite teacher.

Straightening up, Mr. Chad hollered, "That's right, kid, we have class tomorrow, too. Now move along! Hello there, Miss Tibby."

Rollie raced upstairs, pushing past slowpokes along the way. He burst into his bedroom and dove under his bed. He pulled out one of his cardboard boxes and rummaged through it.

He found the marmalade jar with its cryptic tag: *A good snack for the LIBRARY.*

Rollie's instinct had been right about Auntie Ei: she knew more than she appeared to. He turned the jar upside down. His fingers traced an indentation in the bottom of the jar. A three. Rollie jumped to his feet and bumped into a friend.

"Cecily!"

"Rollie, I thought we were partners, but if you want to keep secrets, then go right ahead and keep your secrets."

"I'm not keeping secrets," protested Rollie.

"Then tell me what you discovered in the library." Cecily crossed her arms. "You said something about a jar."

Rollie held up his marmalade jar. "This looks like the same size as those holes in the shelves, right?"

Cecily's green eyes widened. "Right, but why would—"

"Come on!" Rollie bounded downstairs. "Does anyone ever come in here?"

They found the library dark and empty. Rollie made the room bright. He counted the third bookcase from the left, and inspected its side. Yep, a hole. He stuck his hand inside. Yep, a three. He turned his jar over in his hands until the three indentation was right side up like the raised three in the hole. He matched the end of the jar to the hole, and slid it in. A perfect fit. Even the threes matched. But the lip of the jar stuck out. Rollie pushed harder, but it would not go any further. Maybe that was the way it was supposed to fit. He was not sure what to do with the jar now since nothing happened on its own.

"Give it a turn," suggested Cecily in a breathless whisper.

Rollie tried to turn the jar to the left, but it would not budge. He turned to the right—

Click.

Cecily gave a sharp inhale of surprise. Rollie grinned.

The jar turned and the bookcase swayed forward as if on a hinge. They peered behind the yawning bookcase. Through the shadows, they saw more bookshelves carved into the wall. Rows and rows of books crammed the shelves. They did not need to read each of their spines, for they all included the same two words in each of their somewhat varying titles: *Sherlock Holmes.*

"Our missing books!" Rollie gasped. He reached out his hand to grab one off the shelf—

"Hi, roomie! Hey, Cecily."

Rollie and Cecily spun around to see Eliot enter the library. Rollie stepped in front of the open bookcase, and slowly pushed it closed.

Click.

"Trying to solve the Rearranging Library, huh?" Eliot asked.

"Trying. What are you doing here?" His hands behind his back, Rollie slid the jar out of its hole.

Eliot plopped into an armchair. "I thought maybe I should try, too. I'm bored."

"Guess that's what you get for finishing your IS work so early in the morning." Rollie bit his lip. Probably not the nicest thing to say.

Eliot remained unaffected and shrugged. "I guess so. Want to go observe someone? Mr. Notch said it's good practice."

"Oh, uh, we still have our IS work to do," Cecily cut in.

"Shame. See you at dinner."

Rollie ducked out the door, hugging his jar and his thoughts to himself. Cecily followed.

"What have we just discovered?" asked Cecily as they headed upstairs.

"A secret library of sorts," replied Rollie, keeping his voice low as they passed a knot of third-year girls gossiping in the hall. "We better keep this to ourselves for now."

*   *   *   *

Later that night, he lay awake trying to drown out Eliot and Rupert's snores with his own thoughts. So far, it was working since Rollie had a lot to think about. Being alone with his thoughts also muddled his head. Finally he threw aside his covers, flicked on his flashlight, and found his hollow Shakespeare book under his bed. Inside he found his little notepad and pencil stub. He made a list of the Five Ws to record the facts he knew so far, as well as the questions he needed to find answers to.

WHO: Who else knows about the secret
library?

WHAT: My marmalade jar is a key to a
bookcase.

WHERE: The secret shelves have our
Sherlock Holmes books.

WHEN: Sunday night/Monday morning: an
attempted burglary in the library.

WHY: Why does the library rearrange
if the real secret is hidden behind it?

Rollie chewed on the end of his pencil. He felt better after organizing his thoughts on paper. Before he flicked off his flashlight, he jotted down one more question.

P.S. What does Auntie Ei know?

The next morning, Rollie sat at a table on the rooftop, sipping his breakfast tea. His jar of marmalade stood next to his plate of hash browns. He had brought the jar with him hoping to open the secret bookcase during recess. Cecily sat at another table with Tibby, trying to ignore him, but stealing occasional glances his way.

"Marmalade!" Eliot whooped. "That's my favorite! Let me have some for my toast."

Rollie glanced nervously at Eliot, then at his jar. "I haven't taken the wax off yet."

"I know how to pop it off." Eliot gripped a butter knife.

Rollie slid the jar away from Eliot's reach. "I'd rather not share it. It's a gift from my great-aunt."

Eliot's face fell. "Sure, chum." He cast his eyes down to his plate.

Sighing, Rollie slid the jar across the table to Eliot. "Just a little won't hurt—but be careful with it."

"You're a great friend, you know that?" Eliot stabbed the wax with his butter knife, wriggled it around, and plucked out the wax plug. He spread a generous amount on his toast. "Just like home," he sighed with a mouthful. "My nanny got me obsessed with it. I miss her." Sadness crept into his eyes for a moment, but vanished when he took another bite of toast and marmalade.

"Where's your home?" Rollie asked him.

"Edinburgh."

"Scotland?" Rollie asked in surprise. "But you're English, aren't you?"

"My dad works there. My mum died, so I have my nanny. I don't get to go home until Christmas. It's too far for weekend visits."

"I'm sorry, Eliot."

"Don't be. It's the way life is." Eliot finished his toast. "Perfect. Thanks for sharing."

"You can have as much as you want. I'll bring it to breakfast every morning."

"Really? Thanks! I should share something with you."

"You have—your Sherlock Holmes comic books."

"Oh, yeah. Okay, we're even. I didn't really think about it, but I guess you kind of owed me that marmalade."

Rollie let the comment go.

"Guess I'll go brush my teeth." Eliot stood, then sat back down. "Headmaster Yardsly and all the teachers. I forgot it's Tuesday."

Rollie craned his neck around to see the faculty parade out the rooftop door and over to the tables. On Tuesdays, the teachers, including the headmaster, mingled among the students at breakfast time. Headmaster Yardsly thought it important to get to know all the students and make connections with them. Rollie had never known teachers to be so interested in and accessible to their students. It made him feel special.

Mr. Chad sauntered up to Rollie's table, stopping to stand between Rollie and Eliot. "Howdy, sleuths! How do you feel about this Tuesday so far?"

"I think it will be a great Tuesday, Mr. Chad," Rollie replied.

"This marmalade has brightened my day!" Eliot exclaimed.

"Marmalade? Hmm . . . never cared for it much. Nothing beats my mom's strawberry-rhubarb jam."

"Rhubarb?" Rollie could not help making a face.

"I know, sounds gross, but in jam with strawberries, it's scrumptious. To each his own. See you boys later today." Mr. Chad gave them a thumbs-up and moved on to the next table.

Rollie's marmalade turned out to be the conversation topic of the morning. Every teacher commented about it when he or she stopped by to visit.

"Too sweet for my liking, although I am sure one could use the word in a code," Ms. Yardsly pointed out in her firm tone.

"Glass jars preserve wonderful prints!" Miss Hertz twittered, and peered at the jar closely through her magnifying glass.

"Serving marmalade or any other type of spread directly from the jar is poor etiquette, you know," Professor Enches muttered, his teeth clamped down on his pipe.

"I take a little marmalade with my afternoon toast every so often, I do," Mr. Notch rambled, pushing his thick glasses up his nose.

"MARMALADE! Delectable stuff," Headmaster Yardsly boomed.

Rollie watched each teacher closely in hopes of spotting a hint of recognition or knowing towards the marmalade jar. Either they excelled at hiding their thoughts, or they did not suspect that his jar was a key to the secret shelves. As the breakfast hour ended and the faculty returned indoors, Rollie cradled the jar in the crook of his arm and headed to class. Little did he know that his jar had indeed sparked the suspicion of one teacher.

The First Hard Choice

At recess, Rollie raced to the library only to find two fourth-years studying for their history quiz. Books with the titles *Detectives in the Middle Ages*, *Roman Private Eyes*, and *A Complete History of Spies from the Dark Ages* lay open in their laps.

At lunch, Rollie wolfed down his sandwich and milk, much to the annoyance of Cecily, and bounded to the library in hopes of finding it empty. Instead three second-year boys were there arguing about the Rearranging Library. After classes, he poked his head in and found Headmaster Yardsly and Ms. Yardsly engrossed in a hushed discussion. Rollie climbed upstairs, knowing he trailed behind in his Independent Studies and should probably spend the afternoon catching up. He fell asleep that night annoyed.

But he dreamed.

He stood in his bedroom at home. All was quiet, until one by one his family and his teachers and even a few students like Tibby crowded into his room. They admired his telescope, his binoculars, his magnifying glass, and his book collection. Professor Enches said something about it being rude to spy on Mr. Crenshaw from the bedroom window. Then Ms. Yardsly jumped on the bed and bumped her head on the ceiling, which Rollie laughed at. Eliot came late and tried to squeeze into the room, but he could not fit and cried. Rollie felt bad for him. He looked around for Cecily, but she was not there. At one point, he heard a *clink* and saw a hand grab his marmalade jar, knock it against his bed post, and hide it under a handkerchief.

In the morning, Rollie smiled to himself thinking how silly that dream was. He wished he could see Ms. Yardsly jump on a bed. He looked over at Eliot asleep at the desk with his head on top of his books. Rollie stifled a laugh as he reached under his bed for his marmalade jar, but—

"It's gone!"

He buzzed around the room, checking under all three beds and atop the desk cluttered with books and Eliot. He stopped in the center of the tiny room, turning around, looking every which way. He shook Eliot's shoulder.

"The quotient of eighty into three-hundred-and-twenty is four!"

"Eliot, wake up!"

"I wasn't asleep!" snapped Eliot.

"Did you take my marmalade jar?"

Eliot stretched and yawned. "No, but marmalade does sound yummy right now!"

"It's gone."

"What? Where?"

"I don't know. I had it under my bed last night, and when I woke up this morning it was gone."

"Odd, and a pity. I was looking forward to having some with my toast this morning." Eliot closed his books, and pulled on a sweater. "Don't worry about it."

"I should tell Headmaster Yardsly."

"Honestly, Rollie, it's just a jar of marmalade."

It's not just a jar of marmalade.

Rollie sprinted out the door, through the hall, and down the stairs. He did not want to assume too much too soon, but he had an instinct that someone purposely stole his jar knowing it was more than just a jar of marmalade. Rollie's detective mind steamed into full gear.

Who would take it?

The answer did not come easily to him. He tried another question.

Who knew he had it?

That second answer jolted him with a sinking feeling: *practically everyone knew he had it.* Yesterday morning at breakfast every teacher had commented on it, lots of students had seen it, and his roommate had enjoyed it. Too many suspects.

Why had someone stolen it?

That answer did not lend new insight: *obviously to open the secret library.* Rollie's first hunch had been right: the secret library was important.

By now the school day had started as more students emerged from their rooms and made their way up to the roof for breakfast. Some gave Rollie confused looks as he pushed past them in the opposite direction downstairs. He reached Headmaster Yardsly's office on the first floor. Taking a deep breath, he lightly rapped on the door.

"ENTER!"

Rollie opened the door and stepped in. His eyes widened as they took in the office. A fireplace and bearskin rug stole the focus of the room. Two sunken armchairs squatted before it. A mantel clock *tick-tocked* quietly. Several holes initialing V.R. riddled the mantel; Rollie knew revolver bullets had carved those holes a long time ago. A penknife stabbed notes to the mantel. Bookshelves crammed with books flanked either side of the fireplace, which reminded Rollie of Holmes' disorderly method of recording his cases. To the right, in front of a street-side window, loomed a large messy desk. Rollie's eyes roamed around the room to the right corner nearest the door. A homemade chemistry lab hoarded that corner, complete with beakers, test tubes, and a microscope. To his left hung heavy draperies, which Rollie knew concealed a private sitting area. A few items decorated the walls: a violin and bow, an unframed portrait of Henry Ward Beecher, and a little cupboard with a keyhole. Lastly, Rollie recognized a framed black silhouette of a man with a hawk-shaped nose and prominent forehead on the headmaster's desk.

As Rollie stepped into the cozy room, he felt as if he stepped into another world, a fictional world. He had only read about this room, its décor and items, yet he knew it as well as his own bedroom.

"Those are the bullet holes that Holmes made when he practiced shooting his revolver," Rollie said excitedly, pointing to the mantel. "And that's his lab where he studied evidence. Is that really his violin?"

Headmaster Yardsly smiled as he stood behind his desk, his lean frame outlined against the window. "It is. Have you not been here before?"

Rollie shook his head. "I would have visited sooner if I knew your office was Holmes' actual flat. *The* 221b."

"Well then, WELCOME!" the headmaster boomed as usual. "Why are you visiting me this morning?" He sat back down as Rollie approached the desk.

With great effort, Rollie dragged his eyes from his surroundings and focused on his headmaster. "Something of mine was stolen, sir."

Yardsly's eyebrows shot up. "From your room?"

"Yes, sir, last night. When I woke up this morning, it was gone. I can't find it anywhere. I know I had it under my bed last night—"

"HOLD ON!" Yardsly raised his long hand. Back to a normal pitch, he inquired, "What exactly was stolen?"

"My marmalade jar, sir." Rollie watched the headmaster's reaction closely.

Yardsly's keen eyes narrowed slightly as he studied his student. The mantel clock *tick-tocked*, being the only noise in the room for a good five seconds. "Where did you get the jar?"

"My Auntie Ei gave it to me."

At the mention of that name, Yardsly's eyes widened slightly. "Why did your aunt give you a—"

"My great-aunt."

"Why did your GREAT-AUNT give you a jar of marmalade?"

"She said it would be a good snack to enjoy in the *library*," Rollie replied, emphasizing the last word.

Another uneasy five seconds *ticked* by with the headmaster and the student regarding one another.

Finally Yardsly told him, "Step closer, Rollin. No, closer. That's good. Listen carefully: students are not permitted to have marmalade jars in the library. Neither are teachers. Of course stealing is wrong and normally I would address the student body about it. That usually forces the culprit to light. However, a stolen marmalade jar is a dangerous thing. So until I can investigate this, it's best to keep it a secret. Understand?"

Rollie nodded, understanding perfectly what Headmaster Yardsly meant.

"You're a good boy, Rollin, and a fine student, so I hear. You did the right thing coming to me. Now get to breakfast before you miss it."

Rollie turned to go, but stopped and asked, "Does my stolen jar have anything to do with that burglary?"

Headmaster Yardsly rubbed his square chin in thought. "Possibly. You're a fine sleuth."

Smiling, Rollie slipped out the office and raced upstairs to breakfast. He had barely gobbled down his hash browns when the bell rang. Taking one last swig of tea, he hurried off to class. He had a hard time focusing in class because his mind tingled with questions, faces, and guesses.

In Ms. Yardsly's Decoding Course Level One, Rollie jotted down a list of everyone he knew for sure had seen his marmalade jar yesterday. To be safe, he wrote it all in code. He had learned his lesson about leaving things out in the open, even things as trivial-seeming as marmalade jars. At the bottom of the list he added *unknown thief.*

During recess, Rollie searched his room one more time just to be sure the jar really was gone. He found no trace of it.

Rollie was glad Miss Hertz did not make them work in pairs today to analyze prints like she usually did in her Identification of Fingerprint, Footprint, and Ash class. Instead she had them silently read a monograph written by Sherlock Holmes titled *The Tracing of Footsteps.* This gave Rollie more time to mull over his case. He decided that during lunch he would search his room for any "teeny but mighty evidence," referred to by Miss Hertz as prints and dust.

As Professor Enches droned on and on about the proper decorum between a private eye and a member of Scotland Yard in his Spy Etiquette and Interrogation class, Rollie came up with a plan to *politely* interrogate a few classmates who had sat with him the other morning and had seen his jar.

Rollie ate lunch in his room. Munching on his sandwich, Rollie used his magnifying glass to inspect the room. He inspected the door, the doorframe, and the floor. Either he was not as good of a detective as he had hoped, or the burglar was very careful, for he found nothing helpful.

While Mr. Notch acted out a scenario for the students to observe in his Observation class, Rollie thought about doing a little observation of his own. He realized whoever had stolen his jar would want to use it soon. Last time, the burglar had broken into the library during the night. Rollie made plans to hide out in the library that night in hopes of catching the burglar. The idea fluttered in his middle.

Normally Rollie anticipated his last class of the day with Mr. Chad, but today he could not concentrate one the Art of Disguise lesson. He pondered the idea of wearing a disguise of some sort, but he did not really have anything . . .

"Listen, sleuths, you don't need to own a costume shop to disguise yourself. Your own wardrobe holds a lot of disguises. You just have to know how to apply them. Holmes fooled everyone with his disguises because he didn't just wear the part, he *became* the part. He used common clothes and items. So think twice before you throw away that hideous sweater with an embroidered yak that your great-aunt Bertha gave you for Christmas."

In the end, Rollie decided to wear all black. After class, Rollie met Cecily on his way upstairs.

"I need to talk to you," Rollie told her. "Did you take my marmalade jar?"

Cecily stopped on the stairs and glared at him. "Excuse me? Why are you asking me that?"

"Don't get mad. I'm asking everyone if they've seen it or know who—"

"No, you're suspecting me of stealing your jar!" she nearly shrieked. "I'm a suspect to you!"

"Shh!" Rollie glanced nervously around to be sure no one was near enough to hear her. "You're not a suspect—"

"If I wasn't a suspect, then you wouldn't be asking me that! And furthermore, I can't believe after all we've been through together you could even *think* that I would take your jar. Holmes never suspected Watson."

"I'm sorry," Rollie said more out of habit than sincerity. "I'm just covering my bases by asking you. That's what Holmes would do."

Cecily eyed him frostily for a few moments, then turned and flipped her ponytail over her shoulder. Without a word, she took off upstairs.

The Betrayal

"I got you something," Eliot beamed as Rollie entered their room after dinner.

"You did? That's nice of you."

Eliot held something behind his back. "Guess."

"Is it something for school?"

"No. Well . . . kind of. Actually, no."

"Okay. . . . Is it something for fun?"

"Um . . . you could use it for fun, but not really, so no."

"Your clues are confusing." Rollie crossed his arms.

"Give up? Because once you give up I win. That's the rule."

"Sure, I give up."

Eliot held out a sealed jar of orange marmalade. "Here. I noticed you were sad about losing your other one. Plus I really need marmalade on my toast."

Rollie was about to ask why Eliot did not buy himself a jar, but he knew he should say something different. "Thank you, Eliot. That's really kind of you."

"What are friends for?" Eliot shrugged.

Smiling, Rollie agreed. "Yeah, you're a nice friend."

Eliot's face lit up. "I'm glad you've noticed."

* * * *

Rollie turned the doorknob. He paused, gripping the knob in his sweaty palm before opening the door.

Squeak, the door warned quietly.

He stepped into the room and glanced around quickly. The library was cold and dark. Rollie was glad that his black shirt had long sleeves. A pale glow from the street lamp outside illuminated one corner of the library as the light seeped through the one good window. The other window that had been broken was still covered with a board. Rollie stood in the center of the library, pondering his hiding place.

The library did not lend him any good hiding places. There was a decent hiding spot between the armchairs and end table, but that was too near the window. Rollie figured the burglar would enter through a window like before. The only other hiding places were in between the bookcases where Rollie could easily fit. The bookcases were the burglar's targets, but Rollie had no other choice. He crouched between the bookcases closest to the door to be near his escape in case he was discovered. From here he could see the windows and the bookcase that opened with his marmalade jar. That bookcase would be the burglar's first stop. Snug in his hiding place, Rollie tried to calm his breathing.

Inhale, exhale, inhale, exhale.

As much as he tried, he could not slow his racing heartbeat or the insistent flutter in his stomach. He patted his moist palms on his black pants, then wrapped his arms around his knees and hugged them. The last he checked, Eliot's clock read twelve-ten. Rollie guessed it had to be around twelve-twenty now. He hoped the burglar would not be too late . . . if he was coming at all . . .

As the minutes crawled by, Rollie's thoughts trickled into each other, and lead him through a mind maze. He could not allow himself to fall asleep, so he let his mind wander. Often he retraced his thoughts to exercise his deductive reasoning skills because Holmes argued that the ability to reason backwards was invaluable to solving a case. When Rollie retraced his thoughts, he laughed at the way they linked together.

They linked like a chain . . . just like the chain securing a black box to a lamppost down the road from his house. Last winter, he and Cecily had discovered it, and had thought it was the strangest mystery to their neighborhood in a long time. When they asked Mr. Wilson about it, he told them the lamppost had broken, and the contents of that box temporarily kept the lamp operating. Rollie and Cecily had been quite disappointed. It had appeared to be very intriguing, but turned out to be very boring.

In the same way, someone had appeared to be one thing, but had turned out to be a thief who stole Rollie's jar. It had to be someone here at school who noticed his marmalade jar, which meant it was someone appearing to be someone different. A chill prickled up Rollie's spine.

He glanced over at the boarded up window. The first burglar had broken the window to get into the library, which meant the burglar was not someone in the school. So the thief who broke in and the thief who stole his jar were not the same person. Maybe they were working together. Or maybe the two thieves *were* the same person, and he or she had broken the window to make it seem like the work of an outsider.

As much as he wanted to see who the burglar was, he was hesitant to know the truth. He shook his head clear of thoughts. Being a detective meant finding the truth . . . at all costs . . .

Squeak.

Rollie's ears perked up, his heartbeat escalated, and his breathing quickened. He squinted through the gloom at the windows—nothing there. His eyes darted towards the door—it was open!

So far Rollie's assumptions held true that the burglar was someone in the school. Rollie did not recognize the person's face, for it was hidden in shadow beneath a cap. But he did recognize the adult's clothing— his heart nearly stopped. The flutter hardened into a pit in his stomach.

Along with the cap, the intruder wore a dreary coat with an upturned collar. From the glow of the street lamp, Rollie could see a red cravat around his neck.

"By the way, the fun thing about a disguise like that one is that you can be any type of worker and loafer."

As his face heated, Rollie remembered the words of his beloved teacher. As much as he wished it to be untrue, the truth fleshed out before him: the burglar was Mr. Chad in his loafer disguise.

Rollie watched him cross the room to the bookcase numbered three. The thief clutched a marmalade jar with a little tag, and Rollie knew it was his. The loafer fit the marmalade jar in the bookcase's hole, turned the jar, and opened the bookcase. A beam from a flashlight flicked on. With this light, Rollie could see the contents of the secret bookcases. Shelves and shelves of Sherlock Holmes books lined the interior.

The thief grabbed one book and thumbed through it. Unsatisfied, he slid it back into place and grabbed another one. After a few looks through a few books, the burglar found the one he wanted.

When the thief shined his light on the book, Rollie recognized it and almost gasped aloud.

It was his Holmes book. There was no mistaking the distinctive green cover and worn pages.

The burglar tucked the book under his arm.

Click, he pushed the bookcase closed and headed for the door.

He stopped.

He turned.

He stared in Rollie's direction.

Rollie froze.

The burglar turned back to the door and slunk out of the library.

Rollie could not move. He huddled in his hiding place. He wanted to let his thoughts wander, but they would not; they focused on one thing:

Mr. Chad the burglar.

He felt stunned at the truth he had just witnessed. Why did it have to be Mr. Chad, his favorite teacher? *How* could it be Mr. Chad, such a fun and likeable person? How could he steal Rollie's jar? And why had he taken Rollie's Sherlock Holmes book?

There was no way he could know about the telegram Rollie was hiding in his book . . . could he?

Rollie hated that his book—a hiding place for his secret, and a gift from Auntie Ei—was now in the hands of an enemy.

Rollie clenched his hands into fists.

Auntie Ei had given him the marmalade jar. What did Auntie Ei really know? As much as Rollie wanted to funnel blame on his great-aunt, he knew in his heart he had to face the real culprit: his teacher.

With a shaky breath, Rollie stumbled to his feet and quitted the library. He wearily climbed the three flights of stairs back to his floor. With each heavy step, his mind tossed between two choices: turn in Mr. Chad, or ignore the situation and wait for someone else to catch him. Surely Scotland Yard or Headmaster Yardsly would solve the mystery if Rollie could. Rollie did not think he had the strength to report Mr. Chad. Tears stung his eyes as he thought about no more classes with Mr. Chad. Headmaster Yardsly would hire another teacher for the class who would not be as fun—he just knew it.

It was not only the fun that made Mr. Chad his favorite teacher. Mr. Chad had recognized Rollie's detecting skills and had complimented him, saying he had noticed what a fine detective Rollie would make. Had that been a lie too? Rollie had never felt betrayed before.

It hurt.

He crept into bed, pulled the covers up to his chin, and closed his eyes. At first he could not fall asleep. Besides worrying over what to do about Mr. Chad, he worried about his Holmes book and the telegram hidden inside it. He had to get his book back as soon as possible . . .

. . . which meant turning in Mr. Chad.

But right now he couldn't fathom doing that.

Eventually the night's events took toll on him, and he finally drifted off to sleep.

He did not dream.

The Second Hard Choice

"Wake up, sleepy head!" Eliot sang as he pounced on Rollie.

Grumbling, Rollie hid under the covers.

"You're going to miss breakfast. Either way I'm taking that marmalade with me."

"You can have it. I don't care."

Eliot huffed. "Cranky, aren't we? Get up!" He yanked the covers off Rollie.

For a moment, Rollie smiled at his friend's insistence. Then last night's events replayed in his mind, and he frowned. Instead of a flutter in his stomach, he felt a pain. He blinked quickly to fight back the tears welling in his eyes.

"What's the matter with you?" Eliot peered closely at Rollie's blood-shot eyes. "Are you sick? If you're sick, go home. I do *not* want to get sick."

"I'm not sick." Rollie started to undress.

"Why are you wearing all black?"

Rollie grimaced. He forgot what he was wearing. "It's the only thing clean I have right now. I've got to take laundry home this weekend."

"Or you need to pack more. See you upstairs." Eliot bustled out of the room with the jar of marmalade.

Rollie pulled on his trousers and a gray shirt. His hair stuck out every which way, but he did not care. He trudged upstairs to the roof. He took one look at the students eating and chatting and laughing, then turned and went back downstairs. His appetite for food and conversation were gone. Back in his room, he threw himself on his bed and stared up at the ceiling. Alone with his thoughts, he came to a decision: he would not turn Mr. Chad in, not yet anyway. Right now he could not bear to do it. He would mull it over during the weekend and start anew on Monday. In the meantime, he hoped Mr. Chad would not find the telegram hidden in his Holmes book. Maybe there was another reason Mr. Chad had stolen the book.

The rest of the day Rollie felt detached, absent from reality. He attended his classes, took notes, smiled politely at his teachers, and shuffled down the halls with his classmates. No one bothered him and he talked to no one.

He dreaded Disguise class and almost ditched, but did not want to raise Mr. Chad's suspicion. As he watched Mr. Chad be his usual boisterous and humorous self, Rollie knew this was just another disguise the teacher donned. He found it hard to believe that behind the attractive exterior, Mr. Chad was a criminal. For the first time, Rollie was afraid. He had never faced a real criminal before. After class, Rollie navigated to avoid Mr. Chad, hoping not to be stopped at the door. No such luck.

"Rollie, you look awful! You okay?"

His eyes cast down, Rollie nodded. He started perspiring.

"Yeah, right! What's wrong? You can tell me."

Rollie swallowed, his heartbeat quickening. He wanted to demand that Mr. Chad give him back his Holmes book and his marmalade jar. Instead he fibbed, saying, "I'm just a little homesick."

"Don't be embarrassed about that. Even I get homesick. You know what I miss most right now? Pizza! There's this fabulous Italian cafe right down the street from my folks' house. It makes *the* best—"

"Sorry, I need to go." Rollie pulled away, hoping Mr. Chad could not read the terror in his eyes.

* * * *

Friday afternoon finally came. Rollie wanted nothing more than to retreat home and surround himself with his noisy yet comforting family. He also had a thing or two to ask Auntie Ei. He was both disappointed and relieved when the cab driver told him Cecily had taken a separate hansom home. Rollie would have to fix things between Cecily and him.

Although he decided not to turn in Mr. Chad, he did not feel any better. Did he feel badly due to the situation, or because he had made the wrong choice to do nothing?

When Rollie got home at dusk, he found the house quiet and nearly empty. His brothers were still at work, his mother had taken his sisters into town for new shoes, and his father was working late at Regent's College. Rollie dropped his suitcase full of dirty laundry in the entry hall, and headed for his bedroom.

"Sick of stairs," he mumbled as he climbed and climbed. As he passed Auntie Ei's bedroom, he looked back over his shoulder into her open doorway.

"Hello, Rollin," her voice croaked from inside.

Rollie edged into her room. "Hello, Auntie Ei. How are you?"

"Old, of course." Auntie Ei sat in her usual arm-chair by the fire.

"Are you feeling any better?"

"Hardly. No more chocolate for me, I am afraid. How are you?"

"All right, I guess."

Auntie Ei flashed her eyes from the *Daily Telegraph* in her hand to Rollie. "You are a far cry from all right, young man."

Rollie frowned. "Auntie Ei, why did you give me that marmalade jar? Did you know what it was for? Where did *you* get it?"

"Young man, that is an inexcusable number of questions for someone as old as me to answer all at once. I daresay you are upset."

Rollie took a deep breath to calm himself. Straining to keep his voice low, he asked again, "Why did you give it to me?"

"A good question," Auntie Ei approved. "I gave it to you to use. How did you use it?"

"I used it to open the secret library."

"There you have it. I'm afraid there's nothing more mysterious about it," the old woman said very matter-of-factly.

"Yes, there is, Auntie," Rollie countered, surprised at his own assertiveness. "How did you get that jar? Headmaster Yardsly is the only person I know who knows about it."

"If you must know, I am an active member on the Sherlock Academy School Board."

"Really? So it's okay that you have one?"

"There is nothing illegal about having a marmalade jar, Rollin."

"Headmaster Yardsly said those jars are dangerous."

"In the hands of the wrong people, they are. You and I are not *wrong people*."

Tears misted his eyes as he thought about who the *wrong people*, or wrong *person*, were. "Auntie, if someone knows the truth . . . and that someone doesn't say anything about it . . ."

"Go on, Rollin."

"Then is that the same as lying?"

Auntie Ei studied him from behind her spectacles before answering. "I suppose so."

"And that's wrong, right?"

"I haven't the slightest idea why you're asking me. You're an intelligent boy. You ought to know the difference between right and wrong."

Rollie nodded. "It's hard doing the right thing sometimes."

"It almost always is. That's what makes it the right thing. We naturally want to do the wrong thing most of the time."

"Why?"

"The discussion of right versus wrong is a very tedious one, and I don't believe I will live long enough to endure that. Perhaps there's an easier discussion we can engage in."

"I know something about someone. I don't want to say anything about him because I really like him. I want someone else to expose him."

"It sounds very vague, but I respect your privacy. Let me ask you this: you are a detective, correct?" Auntie Ei jabbed a bony finger at him.

"Yes, at least I hope so."

"Rollin, you know very well that you are, and a good one at that. Stop trying to sound modest in this instance, for it comes off as insecurity. You must be confident in who you are without being arrogant—that's modesty. Next question: what does a detective do?"

"I know what a detective—"

"Answer the question, Rollin Edgar Wilson."

"A detective follows clues to solve a mystery and finds out who is guilty."

Auntie Ei nodded her head of gray hair. "There you have it. A detective finds who is guilty and brings that person to justice. Would a detective be doing his job if he discovered the guilty person but never reported him? For example, if an inspector had a lead on Herr Zilch but never acted on it, would he be doing his job?" She smacked the newspaper page bearing the headline *Mayfair Theft Suspected of Being Linked to Herr Zilch*.

Rollie shook his head.

"That detective might as well retire and become a beekeeper! A detective always chooses to do the right thing at any cost; otherwise no one would employ him. Holmes believed that everyone was responsible for preserving justice." Auntie Ei folded the newspaper on her lap.

"So back to the marmalade jar," Rollie began.

"We are through discussing marmalade jars for today. You are excused, Rollin."

Rollie backed into the hallway. He climbed the twelve steps up to his watch-tower room, and sat at his desk by the window overlooking Mr. Crenshaw's garden. Mr. Crenshaw was not there—but Rollie did not feel like spying on him anyway. Instead he looked around at his telescope, his magnifying glass, his notes tacked on the cork-covered wall, and his collection of Sherlock Holmes books. He thought about Auntie Ei's advice.

And he knew what he had to do.

Double Flutters

As the weekend wore on, Rollie felt better. Being around his family gave him the familiar comfort that he needed. Usually he got annoyed with dinnertime, but this weekend he relished it, realizing he missed his family member's interruptions and teasing. Still something was not quite right.

Cecily.

He called on her Saturday, but found she was not at home. He tried again Sunday afternoon. At first she did not want to see him, but when he persisted at the front door, she reluctantly met him on the porch. They sat together on the front porch steps.

"What do you want? I'm right in the middle of homework." she said crossly.

"Homework?" Rollie raised his eyebrows. "We don't have homework."

Cecily blushed. In a small voice, she confessed, "I didn't finish my IS for the week."

"I didn't know you could take unfinished work home."

"I'm not sure you can. I'm being sneaky about it."

Rollie gave her a disapproving look.

Cecily rolled her green eyes. "I'll talk to Headmaster about it first thing Monday morning."

"Guess we'll both be bothering him first thing Monday morning." Rollie took a deep breath. "I need to tell you what I've been up to."

"About time." Cecily muttered.

"I'm sorry for keeping secrets from you." said Rollie, shifting uncomfortably.

He told her about his stake out in the library. Cecily's eyes widened when he concluded that Mr. Chad was the burglar, and that he had stolen Rollie's jar and Holmes book.

"That makes me sad," she sighed. "I really like him."

"He's my favorite teacher, but I know the right thing to do is turn him in," said Rollie quietly. "I should have told you about this sooner. And I shouldn't have suspected you of taking the jar. Sorry."

Cecily smiled. "No harm done. I mean, besides hurting my feelings for a little bit. You know, for as much as I love Holmes, I never liked how he left Watson out of the loop. I felt like Watson this week."

"Well, I'm not Holmes and you're not Watson. I'm Rollie and you're my best friend Cecily. That's all that matters." Rollie socked her shoulder playfully.

When Rollie left Cecily's house and headed down the street to his, he spotted Mr. Crenshaw strolling toward him. He raised a hand in greeting, and met Mr. Crenshaw in front of the Wilson house.

"Good afternoon, young man," Mr. Crenshaw smiled, his face creasing into many wrinkles. Although it was a pleasant day, the elderly man wore a long gray coat and his gloves. "I was just on my way over to your house to ask if you wouldn't mind delivering another letter to Ichabod." He held out a long envelope.

"Sure." Rollie took the envelope.

"I realize I may have inconvenienced you with this task," said Mr. Crenshaw in a kindly tone, "but you are greatly appreciated."

Rollie looked up at Mr. Crenshaw in skepticism. "Is this really all about a surprise party?"

Mr. Crenshaw's jaw tightened, and he seemed to be weighing something in his mind. "Very well, young man. I suppose you have earned the right to know. But what I am about to disclose to you must be kept secret—you know, from one detective to another, eh?" He leaned in closer to Rollie. "I work for a top secret division of Scotland Yard. Ichabod Enches is my fellow agent who's been planted at Sherlock Academy to uncover an enemy spy."

Rollie was about to mention the recent break-in and ask if that was the work of the enemy spy, but Mr. Crenshaw continued.

"The only way for the two of us to communicate is through letters delivered by you. We can't risk the letters getting intercepted in the post, and we can't trust any of the adults—including the headmaster—at the Academy until we uncover the spy. It is of the utmost importance that you keep our secret, even from your family." Mr. Crenshaw gave a thin smile. "You are doing a great service in helping the Yard."

Rollie said, "I'll keep your secret, sir. You can trust me."

Mr. Crenshaw beamed down at him. "I knew I could trust you. Indeed you are becoming a fine detective. We'll be in touch." With a wink, he turned and hobbled back to his mansion.

Rollie stood on his front walkway, eyeing the envelope in his hands. He held it up to the sunlight. The stationary was too thick to see through. Curiosity gnawed at Rollie; he wanted to read what was inside. Perhaps there were facts inside that could tie Mr. Chad to the enemy spy. He almost ripped it open, but shook his head. Nope, that could jeopardize Scotland Yard's mission to find the spy.

He was surprised to learn that Mr. Crenshaw was a Yard inspector, yet it made sense. It explained his frequent trips away, the cryptic documents he kept in his briefcase, and his interest in Rollie as a detective. Rollie felt jolted to learn there was an enemy spy hiding at the school, but that made sense in light of the library break-ins and his stolen marmalade jar. He felt his stomach tighten as he remembered who the enemy spy most likely was, and he realized he should tell Mr. Crenshaw about Mr. Chad. He started toward the mansion next door.

He stopped. Something felt off.

Mr. Crenshaw and Professor Enches did not trust any adults at the school, not even Headmaster Yardsly. They were going out of their way by trusting Rollie in order to avoid Yardsly knowing about their letters. Sure, they could consider the headmaster a suspect for the enemy spy. But even if Rollie did not know the spy was Mr. Chad, he would still not suspect Yardsly for one simple fact: Auntie Ei trusted him, and had told Rollie to do the same. And in turn, Rollie trusted Auntie Ei.

Rollie headed back to his house. He decided to consult Headmaster Yardsly before consulting Mr. Crenshaw. Yardsly would handle this mystery better. Besides, there was something about Mr. Crenshaw that Rollie did not entirely trust, and he was learning not to discount his instincts.

At dinner that night, the family conversation bantered away as usual.

"Fact: another week is upon us," Mr. Wilson began.

"Alice is leaving town," Stewart whined, gnawing on his drumstick.

"The family's been warned! Stew will be moping around for the next week," Edward joked.

"Why is Alice leaving town?" Mrs. Wilson asked, passing Daphne the rolls.

"Holiday with her folks."

"Daddy," Lucille piped up. "When can we go on holiday?"

"We just went on holiday in June."

"That was a long time ago!"

"Fact: two months is not a long time ago, darling."

"To me it is."

"Let's talk about this week," said Mr. Wilson, changing the subject. "Fact: September is fast upon us. Oh, Rollie, what will you be doing this week?"

"Doing the right thing," Auntie Ei cut in, nodding knowingly at Rollie.

"Auntie's right, Dad."

"That's good to hear. Fact: doing the right thing always pays off." Mr. Wilson raised his glass to toast this wise saying.

* * * *

"Are you ready then?" Cecily asked on Monday morning as she and Rollie bumped along in their horse-drawn cab.

"Yes," Rollie said resolutely.

The hansom pulled up to 221 Baker Street, and Rollie and Cecily hopped out. They mounted the front steps and entered the school. It was relatively quiet—a difference from last Monday morning when they had arrived at a crime scene. Embarking upon their third week at the Academy, they felt at home as they entered the entry hall. They both stepped up to the headmaster's door and knocked together.

Ms. Yardsly opened the door. She stood tall with her hands behind her back. Her hair was twisted into its tight bun and her brown suit looked crisper than ever, as did her expression.

"Can I speak with Headmaster?" Rollie ventured to ask.

Ms. Yardsly stood aside and ushered the two children into the office.

"GOOD MORNING!" the headmaster greeted from behind his desk. "How can I help you two on this fine Monday?"

Rollie quickly told the two Yardslys about his investigation in the library, how he had witnessed the thief open the secret shelves and steal his book, and his suspicion that Mr. Chad was the culprit. Both Yardslys were extremely shocked by all he had to share.

"I must confess Chadwick was the last person on my suspects list," Ms. Yardsly said.

Headmaster Yardsly stood from his chair. "I agree, but Rollie presents some good facts we cannot ignore. We'll take Chadwick into custody and interrogate him immediately. Now get to class." He picked up the telephone and dialed.

"One more thing, sir," Cecily spoke up in a small voice. She told him about taking her IS work home to finish.

Headmaster Yardsly sighed. "IS work is not usually accepted late, but in light of your good detective work we'll excuse it just this once."

As Rollie and Cecily left the office, they heard Headmaster Yardsly speaking on the telephone with an inspector from Scotland Yard.

"I'm glad that's over with," Rollie blew out a breath. "I'm sick of carrying this secret around."

"What secret?" a new voice cut in.

Rollie saw Eliot coming toward them down the hall.

"Hey, Eliot, how was your weekend?"

"What secret?"

"If I told you, it wouldn't be a secret."

"Cecily knows," Eliot argued.

"It's just a secret between us."

Eliot's face portrayed hurt feelings.

Cecily jumped in. "Actually, Eliot, it's about my parents. They're not getting along right now. I'm a little sensitive about it."

Eliot's face softened. "Sorry, Cecily. That's too bad. I won't pry."

"Thank you, Eliot. Breakfast?"

The three students headed up to the roof for breakfast. When Eliot got lost in the crowd, Rollie leaned over to Cecily and whispered, "Thanks for that, but you didn't have to lie for me."

"I didn't lie. I told the truth."

Rollie frowned. "I'm sorry. I didn't know that—"

"Never mind. I guess that's why I was a little more sensitive this week than usual."

"You should have told me."

"Well, I would have, but you were busy with this case." She smiled and playfully socked his shoulder.

Rollie smiled back at her sheepishly and promised himself to include her in the rest of his detective work. He was glad that she had forgiven him so easily, but he was still worried about his other problem.

Although Rollie knew he had done the right thing by turning in Mr. Chad, he did not feel any better.

Rollie felt sickly flutters in his middle when he and Cecily spotted Inspectors Pembly and Clyde enter Mr. Chad's classroom. The students gawked as Mr. Chad was handcuffed and escorted downstairs by the inspectors. Rollie watched them leave the Academy, and he felt sad all over again. It was still hard to believe that, behind that jovial façade, Mr. Chad was a thief and an enemy. Rollie marveled at how well Mr. Chad had disguised himself, and found himself respecting the American teacher for his skills. At least Mr. Chad had practiced what he preached: he had not only worn the part, he had truly *become* the part and had fooled everyone.

Just as Rollie wondered who would take over Mr. Chad's Disguise class, he saw Ms. Yardsly post a sign on Mr. Chad's classroom door that read *Disguise Class Canceled Until Further Notice.*

This made Rollie feel even worse.

"You did the right thing, you know," Cecily told them as they headed into Ms. Yardsly's classroom.

The week continued on. There was no word about Mr. Chad, and Disguise class stayed canceled. Rollie wanted to ask Headmaster Yardsly about Mr. Chad's interrogation, but Yardsly spent the next few days at Scotland Yard questioning Mr. Chad. Rollie was anxious to get his book and his marmalade jar back, and wondered if they had been found yet. In the midst of Mr. Chad's arrest, Rollie had forgotten to deliver Mr. Crenshaw's letter to Professor Enches until the professor asked him after class on Thursday if there was any word from Mr. Crenshaw. Rollie promised to retrieve the letter from his room and get it to Enches after classes.

When he returned to Enches' classroom with the letter in hand, Rollie found the classroom empty and dark. He flicked on the light and padded between the desks and chairs. Professor Enches' desk was as tidy as ever. Rollie placed the envelope in the center of the desk so he would see it as soon as he sat down. Rollie turned to leave, but stopped when something caught his eye. Something red and frayed peeked out from underneath the desk.

Rollie stooped for a closer look. He reached out his fingertips and grabbed it.

A red cravat.

In one second, Rollie felt a flutter of sickish surprise. He knew right away it was Mr. Chad's disguise, but what was it doing under Professor Enches' desk? Did this indicate that Professor Enches was the disguised culprit Rollie had seen in the library?

Rollie started to feel relieved.

Or had Mr. Chad stashed it under the professor's desk to pass the blame onto him? Rollie felt queasy again.

Rollie needed more evidence before he could decide on a conclusion. Holmes always warned against relying on circumstantial evidence, and impressed the importance of details. Was there a detail Rollie was missing?

He reviewed Mr. Crenshaw's story about being undercover for Scotland Yard. If his story was true, then why did Enches have Mr. Chad's disguise hidden in his desk? If his story was false, then who exactly were Mr. Crenshaw and Professor Enches? There had to be a way to corroborate or disprove Mr. Crenshaw's story about working undercover for Scotland Yard. But how?

The letter.

Stuffing the red cravat back under the desk, Rollie reached for the letter. The other day curiosity had almost compelled him to open the letter, but today desperation drove him to tear it open. The contents of the letter would reveal Mr. Crenshaw's and Enches' motives. He stood with his back to the door as he stared at the envelope in his hands, wondering if he should open the letter right there or take it up to his room.

"Good afternoon, Rollin E. Wilson."

A New Hat

Rollie jumped. When he spun around, he was face to face with Professor Enches. The professor clasped his hands behind his back, puffed on his pipe, and smiled down at the boy.

"What brings you to my classroom this late in the afternoon?" he asked in a friendly tone.

"I, uh, was just delivering your letter." With a shaky hand, Rollie held out the envelope to the professor.

Professor Enches took it. "Thank you, lad."

"I was just about to leave it on your desk like you asked me to."

Professor Enches stood in front of the door as he opened the letter, blocking Rollie's path of escape. Rollie swallowed and blinked. The professor looked up and nodded at him. Although Rollie had no reason to feel guilty, he felt his stomach churning. Finally, Professor Enches stepped aside to let Rollie exit. Once through the door, Rollie ran downstairs, not stopping until he reached the headmaster's office. Panting outside the door, he rapped on it, hoping the headmaster was back from Scotland Yard.

"ENTER!"

Relieved, Rollie barged into the office. "Headmaster! I was wrong about Mr. Chad! He's innocent. It's Professor Enches!" He told him about finding the red cravat under Enches' desk.

Yardsly's straggly eyebrows rose. "How do we know the cravat was worn by Enches, and wasn't planted under his desk by Chadwick?"

Rollie swallowed. "I just know it."

Yardsly sighed. "A good detective heeds his instincts. HOWEVER, he also analyzes the evidence and searches the facts for the truth. We need more evidence before we release Chadwick and arrest Enches." When he noticed Rollie's fallen countenance, he added quickly, "BUT I will question Ichabod about the cravat under his desk."

Rollie left the office. He suspected Professor Enches was the culprit; yet Rollie did not want to be a detective who acted on feelings. Still he had an instinct, and so far his instincts had served him well. But Headmaster Yardsly was right: Rollie needed to build a stronger case. He needed more evidence. His instinct told him that evidence was in that letter from Mr. Crenshaw.

Getting that letter would be tricky.

He needed help. He needed his Watson.

*　*　*　*

The next day, Rollie and Cecily had their plan formed and ready for implementation. Rollie did not know if Yardsly had questioned Enches about the cravat yet, or if Mr. Chad had been released from Scotland Yard; his disguise class was still canceled. But Rollie was not about to waste any more time before gathering evidence to support his suspicion of Professor Enches.

At eleven-thirty, Rollie filed into his Etiquette class with the other students and took his usual seat. Professor Enches stood up from his desk and began his lecture. Rollie appeared to be listening intently by keeping his eyes on the professor, and jotting down a few notes here and there. Cecily's chair stood vacant. Suddenly, the classroom door creaked open and Cecily's head popped in.

"Excuse me, professor," Cecily called in a little voice. "May I please speak with you for just a moment, sir? It's extremely important." She looked like she might cry, so the professor hurried over to her.

All the students turned their heads to see the disturbance. That was exactly what Rollie had hoped for. In a blink, he was behind the professor's desk, opening drawers and searching for the letter.

"I'm very upset about this . . . right now . . . and I just—" Cecily burst into loud wails.

"There, there, now, tears are no proper form of etiquette, and I can't help you unless I know exactly what the problem is."

Frantically, Rollie shuffled through the desk drawers. He slid them closed just as he noticed the professor's briefcase on the floor—a thick parchment envelope stuck out. Rollie snatched it and stuffed it under his shirt as one scrawny boy in the front spotted him. The boy gaped, mouth ajar. Rollie put his finger to his lips, hoping the boy would understand his signal and not give him away.

But the boy was just like Rollie, and thought it his duty to report any crimes.

"Professor Enches!"

The professor spun around as Rollie reached his seat.

"Professor Enches! He was behind your desk!" the little boy announced, pointing an accusing finger at Rollie.

Rollie paled as the professor marched over to him.

"Rollin E. Wilson, no student is allowed behind a teacher's desk." He barked at Rollie, his mustache twitching. "Class dismissed!"

Murmurs of confusion stirred.

"This instant!" the professor demanded.

Students scrambled out of their seats and pushed through the door. Rollie hurried after them, but got caught by Enches' hand. Cecily cast him a terrified expression as she was herded out by her peers. The door slammed shut.

Professor Enches gripped Rollie's collar, yanked him over to a nearby chair, and pushed him into it. He eyed Rollie closely. Enches' flushed complexion faded and his breathing slowed as he regained his composure.

Rollie sat very still as if any sudden movement might trigger the professor's temper. He also did not want to betray the envelope hidden beneath his shirt. Seconds dragged into minutes as the teacher and student silently regarded one another. Finally, Enches broke the thick silence.

"Why were you behind my desk?" he asked, attempting to keep his voice under control.

Rollie gulped.

"Rollin, it's bad etiquette to not answer your elders."

"I have my reasons, sir," Rollie managed with more courage than he thought he had.

"You are a bright lad, but I am smarter still. I know what you were after."

Rollie tried to read the professor's expression. Was he bluffing in hopes of Rollie confessing? Or did he suspect Rollie of knowing the truth? Rollie mustered more courage and tried to bait back.

"Sir, why don't you report me to Headmaster?"

Professor Enches' mustache twitched again. "I do not wish to inconvenience Headmaster. I'm sure you and I can resolve this properly."

He knows that I know, Rollie realized with dread. His only safety was the headmaster. If he could convince Enches to turn him in—

"Listen, lad, I do not want us to be enemies. If you confess your theft, I will spare you punishment. Mr. Crenshaw and I have trusted you with our secret operation to uncover the enemy spy. I thought you were on our side."

Rollie found himself believing the professor, and believing in the high regard Enches and Mr. Crenshaw had for him. Maybe he had assumed too quickly that Enches was the guilty player in this mystery. Perhaps he should hand over the letter . . .

"Be wise and tell me the truth," Enches coaxed in a gentler tone.

No. Whether the letter incriminated or exonerated Enches, it was too valuable to give up. Rollie would not possess evidence like this again. He had to keep it, and he had to get it to Headmaster Yardsly . . . at all costs.

Rollie's demeanor changed. His jaw clenched firmly, his gaze hardened, and his body stiffened with resolution. He suddenly felt brave.

The professor noticed.

"Don't be stubborn, Rollin," he said. "If you will not help us uncover the enemy spy then—"

"But I *have* uncovered the enemy spy," retorted Rollie. "*You.*"

With shocking speed, Enches lunged forward and pinned Rollie's arms to his sides with an iron grip, putting his face inches from Rollie's. The professor's grandfatherly façade melted away.

In a vehement whisper, Enches threatened, "You are no match for us. You have no idea who you are dealing with. You *will* cooperate."

Rollie trembled, but bravely held his teacher's gaze. Rollie's arms tingled as if they were falling asleep, so tight was Enches' grip on them.

Rollie could feel hot breath against his cheeks. He tried to wiggle free, but immediately regretted it. The envelope made a crinkling sound under his shirt. Enches heard it.

Enches whipped the envelope out from under Rollie's shirt. "Thief!" he hissed. "You will go straight to the headmaster now!"

"No, *you're* the thief!" Rollie shot back. "You broke into the library, but discovered the secret bookcases opened only with a marmalade jar. So you stole mine and used it to open the secret bookcase. You stole my Holmes book. And you used Mr. Chad's disguise to do it."

Professor Enches released his grip on Rollie and stood up. "You're cleverer than we anticipated, but you'll never be a match for us."

He rushed to the window and threw it up. He dug inside the inner pocket of his tweed jacket and threw something at his feet.

BANG!

Hissssss!

Without a second thought, Rollie hit the floor and covered his head with his hands.

He did not hear any more explosions, so he lifted his head and opened his eyes. A column of black smoke filled the room, completely hiding the professor.

The smoke stung Rollie's eyes and made him cough. As the smoke wafted out the open classroom window, Rollie looked around for Enches. There was no sign of him.

Rollie bolted up and scrambled to the window. He saw Enches climbing down the fire escape ladder. Rollie ducked out the window and slid down the ladder just as Enches landed in the alley below. Rollie fell off the ladder. He picked himself up, and barely saw Enches running down the alley toward the back of the school building.

Rollie took off. He had no idea how he was going to stop Enches from escaping—he just knew he had to.

Enches disappeared around the back of the building. Rollie skidded around the corner.

Enches was heading for Baker Street. Rollie knew once the professor reached the bustling street it would be nearly impossible to catch him due to all the pedestrians and traffic. Rollie was losing the chase.

A man suddenly jumped out into the alley and tackled Enches to the ground.

"Ahhhh!" Professor Enches roared.

Rollie reached them as the man pinned Enches down with his arms behind his back. Rollie snatched the envelope from Enches' hand.

"Going somewhere, prof?" Mr. Chad quipped as he held Enches down. "Hey, kiddo!" he nodded at Rollie.

A wave of relief flooded Rollie as he grinned at Mr. Chad. There was no doubt in Rollie's heart regarding

Mr. Chad's true innocence now. Relief turned to gratitude; gratitude that Mr. Chad was innocent, gratitude that he had returned, and gratitude that, above all, he had stopped Enches from escaping.

"Do me a favor, huh?" Mr. Chad panted as Enches struggled to break free. Although the professor was tall, he was no match for Mr. Chad's youth and strength. "Go tell Yardsly what's up. We need some cops down here fast."

Wasting no time, Rollie darted back down the alley, around to the front of the school building, and through the front door. He pounded on the headmaster's office door.

"ENTER!"

Rollie barged in. "Headmaster, Mr. Chad's got him! Hurry, before he gets away!"

"ROLLIN! What on earth are you talking about?" Yardsly asked as he shot to his feet from behind his desk. "CALM YOURSELF! What do you need to tell me?"

Rollie swallowed and collected his thoughts. He quickly related Enches' confession and attempted escape. He slapped the letter onto Yardsly's desk.

Headmaster Yardsly called Scotland Yard on the telephone, and then followed Rollie to where Mr. Chad had Enches pinned down.

"Great job, both of you!" Yardsly told Mr. Chad and Rollie. He squatted down next to Enches. "I believe you have quite an explanation to give, Professor."

* * * *

Throughout the rest of the day, Rollie kept quiet about his involvement in Enches' arrest and kept his questions to himself. He did not want to bother the headmaster about the case. The faculty had been occupied with the arrest, but he still wanted to know how the puzzle pieces fit together. That evening after supper, Yardsly summoned Rollie to his office.

With a flutter of excitement, he skipped downstairs to the headmaster's office.

"Rollin, my dear detective, take a seat." Headmaster Yardsly waved to the left armchair in front of the crackling fireplace.

Rollie eased into the worn but comfy armchair, remembering Dr. Watson always sat on the left. He felt privileged to sit in Watson's chair.

"I suppose you'd like to know the rest of the mystery, am I right?"

Rollie nodded. "I have some of the mystery solved, but I don't know who Mr. Crenshaw and Enches really are and what they were after in the Rearranging Library."

"How did you know Enches was the library thief?"

Rollie told him about his plan to swipe Mr. Crenshaw's letter because he believed it was evidence that Enches was the culprit. He related his confrontation with the professor, which had led to Enches' confession and arrest.

"Why are our Holmes books hidden in the secret library?" asked Rollie.

"A profile of each student is kept in his or her personal volume. That profile includes personal information like home address and IQ scores. More importantly, we hold profiles on past students who are currently serving their country as policemen, detectives, and spies. That's the reason we hide the books in the secret shelves. We use the Rearranging Library as a decoy. Remember, appearances can be deceiving." He beamed, and added, "Honestly, it's great fun watching students pull their hair out over the Rearranging Library!"

Rollie chuckled. "It's a good decoy. So Enches wanted my profile hidden in my Holmes book." He didn't want to mention his telegram. "What was he going to do with it?"

"He was going to give it to the man he was working for."

"Mr. Crenshaw," said Rollie. "Who's not a Yard agent after all, right? Who's he really?"

186

"That answer was in the letter you delivered from Mr. Crenshaw to Enches. My sister—er, Ms. Yardsly worked hard to decode it. It turns out that your neighbor Mr. Crenshaw has been disguising himself as an elderly gentleman. But he is actually Herr Zilch."

Rollie gasped. "*The* Herr Zilch? The Herr Zilch constantly in the papers?"

"THE SAME! The same Herr Zilch who has been untraceable for years. Apparently he took on the name Mr. Crenshaw, and was living in disguise next door to you."

"I can't believe it!" Rollie nearly laughed. "Wait till Auntie Ei hears about this."

Yardsly smiled. "INDEED! Herr Zilch is the leader of a secret organization known as M.U.S., which stands for Moriarty's Underground Society. Professor Moriarty founded this secret society long ago. I assume you're familiar with him."

"Of course, sir! He was Holmes' greatest enemy. He was called the Napoleon of crime. Holmes actually respected him because he was so brilliant."

"EXACTLY! He was Holmes' ultimate nemesis. M.U.S. continues as a crime league under Zilch's leadership."

"And Enches is a member of M.U.S," said Rollie.

Headmaster Yardsly nodded. "It turns out that Ichabod was Herr Zilch's spy planted here at the

Academy. We monitor all mail, telegrams, and telephone calls here—we're always on guard against Herr Zilch. So they communicated through letters delivered by a private courier. "

Rollie felt horrified. "Me! I was helping them all along!"

"Calm yourself, lad. You had no idea. They were using you, yes, but that turned out to be their undoing," said Headmaster Yardsly.

Rollie got excited by a sudden thought. "You know where Zilch is now! Next door to me. You can arrest him!"

The headmaster rubbed his temples wearily. "Yet again he evades us. By the time Scotland Yard got to his house this afternoon, Herr Zilch was gone. Scotland Yard is searching his house for fingerprints and clues, and will put it under acute surveillance in case Zilch returns."

"He won't return though," Rollie said.

"Most likely not," muttered Yardsly. "For now, what matters is that the secret library is safe, and you are the school hero."

"Hero?"

Headmaster Yardsly reached down beside his chair and brought up a box that he dropped on Rollie's lap. "For you, in appreciation for your services and to remind you that you're a fine detective."

Rollie pried the lid off and grinned. He took out a plaid felt hat with earflaps tied on the top. It was a deerstalker hat like the one that Sherlock Holmes always wore in the illustrations of him. He put it on.

"Usually we award these deerstalker hats to upperclassmen who solve fieldwork cases, but you've earned it," Headmaster Yardsly commented with a wink.

"Thank you, sir, thank you very much."

"One thing, Rollie, and I am sorry to require this of you. Our conversation here today must be kept a secret."

"May I tell my friend Cecily? She helped me get the letter, and she knows everything up to this point. She's my Watson, after all."

Headmaster Yardsly considered. "VERY WELL. Only your Watson, no one else."

"I have a question, sir." Rollie adjusted the hat on his head. "What did Mr. Crenshaw's letter say?"

"I'd like to tell you, Rollie, but I must meet with my staff first. There are a few things we need to discuss before I share that with you."

"Yes, sir." Smiling, Rollie jumped to his feet and bounded to the door. He paused and turned. "Did you find my book and my marmalade jar yet?"

"No need to worry. We recovered them from his desk. Your book is safe and sound in the secret library again. I've also taken the liberty of locking up your marmalade jar with mine. Better safe than sorry."

Rollie heaved a sigh of relief. "Good. I was worried about my book."

Headmaster Yardsly pursed his thin lips. "I suppose you know there was another reason Enches stole your book, right?"

Rollie eyed his headmaster. "Yeah—I kept something valuable in my book. I don't know how Enches knew about it or why Herr Zilch would want it."

Yardsly studied his student closely. Hesitantly he asked, "What did you keep in there?"

At first Rollie wasn't going to tell him, but he remembered how Auntie Ei had vouched for Yardsly and trusted him completely. Rollie relented. "I have an original telegram from Holmes to Watson that Auntie Ei bought for me at an antiques auction. I use it as my bookmark. It's worth some money."

Yardsly's face relaxed and he chuckled. "So that's the secret in your book, eh? A good thing we recovered it."

"But how did Enches and Zilch know about it? And why would they care about it?"

Yardsly hesitated before saying, "I'm not entirely sure, but apparently you're someone worth keeping an eye on."

Ring-ring!

Yardsly answered his telephone. Rollie was about to leave the office when Yardsly stopped him.

"It's your father. Your aunt Eileen is very sick," Yardsly told him, covering the mouth piece as he spoke. "Some sort of stomach problem."

"She hasn't been feeling well. She needs to stop eating those chocolates Mr. Crenshaw sent . . ." Rollie trailed off.

Yardsly listened on the telephone, then covered the mouth piece again and said to Rollie, "Your father says to head home. They may need to take her to the hospital."

"Thank you, sir." Rollie left the office, and ran into Cecily near the front door. He quickly told her about Auntie Ei, and as he did, a thought struck his brain, which morphed into a pit that weighted his stomach.

"It's probably just a stomach bug," Cecily assured him.

"No." Rollie shook his head. "She's been poisoned."

"*Poisoned?*" Cecily gaped at him.

"Zilch has been poisoning her!" exclaimed Rollie. With that, he ran outside and jumped into the first hansom he saw.

Elementary

"Can you go any faster?" Rollie yelled up at the driver. The driver flicked his reins, and the horse pulling the hansom picked up his pace.

Rollie's stomach had never fluttered so badly, and he kept taking deep breaths to try to calm himself. It wasn't working. The drive home seemed to take an eternity, but eventually the hansom pulled up in front of the Wilson manor.

Rollie forgot to thank the driver as he bolted out of the hansom and dashed up the front walkway to his house. He met his father on the stairs.

"Dad! How is Auntie Ei?" Rollie panted as he ran past his father up to the second floor.

"Fact: she's not doing too well. She's eighty-something years old, and we may need to face the fact that her time to go may—"

"No, Dad! She's been poisoned! She needs to go to the hospital!" Rollie hurried into Auntie Ei's bedroom without knocking.

He found his great-aunt lying in bed. By the dim light of her bedside lamp, she looked very pale. He padded over to her and rested a hand on her cold wrinkled one.

Her eyelids fluttered open. "Rollin, what are you doing here?" she croaked.

Rollie quickly told her about Mr. Crenshaw being Herr Zilch, and how he was sure Zilch had poisoned those chocolates. He expected her to argue with him, or even scoff at his theory.

Instead she gripped his hand and said, "Listen to me very carefully and do exactly as I say." She took a shallow breath. "In that cabinet you will find a collection of substances."

Rollie looked across the room where she was pointing.

"For heaven's sake, go open it!" Even in her weakened condition Auntie Ei could snap at him.

Rollie scurried over to the small cabinet hanging next to the fireplace. He opened it, and found its shelves crammed with little bottles full of different colored liquids.

"What do you need?" he called to her.

"The bottle of green liquid marked with the number ten." Auntie Ei took another breath. "And the bottle of pink liquid marked with a seven. And the bottle marked with fourteen that looks like it is full of black sand. Do you see them? Ten, seven—"

"I got them!" Rollie snapped back as he carried the three bottles back to her bedside. "What'll I do with them?"

Auntie Ei closed her eyes, and her breathing became very shallow. Rollie panicked and shook her shoulder.

She jolted and opened her eyes. She looked slightly annoyed, but was too weak to chide him. "Mix the three together. Use my tea cup." Her words came out in wheezy gasps.

Rollie grabbed her tea cup off the end table. He pulled out the stoppers from all three bottles. He was about to ask her how much to mix from each bottle, but when he glanced at her he knew there wasn't much time left for questions like that. She was fading quickly. He poured all the green and pink liquids and black sand into the tea cup. He used his finger to stir the substances together, then lifted the tea cup to her face.

"Auntie Ei! Open your mouth! You've got to drink this right now!" His voice sounded high.

She opened her mouth a little. He brought the tea cup to her thin lips and tipped the antidote into her mouth. She drank, choked, coughed, and drank some more. Once she drained the cup, she sighed.

Rollie watched her intently. He wanted her to open her eyes, or take a deep, healthy breath, or snap at him—anything to show that she was out of danger and that she would be fine and go on to live forever so he wouldn't be alone and—

"Rollin," she croaked.

"Did it work? Are you alright?"

Auntie Ei smiled slightly. "I believe so."

"How did you know which antidote to use?" Rollie shook his head in awe.

"This is the not first time I have been poisoned, and I daresay it won't be the last." Auntie Ei smiled a little wider. "I know a thing or two about Frederick Zilch, such as his poison of choice. He should know that two can play at this game."

* * * *

Once Auntie Ei was fully recovered, she made Rollie tell her all about the burglary at the Academy, about Enches, and about Mr. Crenshaw. She scolded herself for not seeing through his disguise and figuring out that he was Herr Zilch. She hated that he had been living right next door to her all along, and no one was the wiser. Rollie was too relieved that she had not succumbed to the poison to be upset about it.

Rollie found himself quite the celebrity when he returned to Sherlock Academy the next week. When Headmaster Yardsly had given that deerstalker hat to Rollie, he did not make life easier for the boy. The upperclassmen were amazed that a first year had received such an honorable award. Wesley Livingston mentioned that Rollie was the youngest student ever to have earned one. Naturally everyone wanted to know why Rollie had been given the hat. The short answer he gave was "It was a thank-you gift for helping him with a problem." That answer only led to more questions, usually ending with why Ichabod Enches had left the Sherlock Academy. As the week wore on, however, the students grew bored with the whole thing and gave up pestering Rollie. Except for Eliot.

"Can you get me one of those hats, ol' bean?" he asked while the two boys finished their math homework after supper on Thursday evening. Eliot consented to studying with Rollie in the evenings since he kept falling asleep at dawn.

Ignoring his roommate, Rollie finished his long division.

"Did you hear me?" Eliot persisted.

"Yes, but the answer is no."

"Then tell me how to get one. What kind of problem do I need to help with?"

Rollie erased his answer. He had divided wrong. "I'm not sure. Just keep your eyes open for problems, I guess."

"I need more details, you know? Personal problems with the headmaster? Or maintenance problems with the building? Which reminds me. Our faucet is dripping. If there's one thing I can't stand it's a dripping faucet. All I hear is drip, drip, drip, drip, drip—"

"And all I can hear is yack, yack, yack from my roomie."

"Sorry, chum, but it really annoys me. And I won't rest till it's fixed, or till I get one of those—"

Rollie tossed the hat to him. "You can borrow it."

"Thanks!" Eliot adjusted it on his head and went to the bathroom to admire it in the mirror. "I think it suits me better."

"Of course you do," Rollie muttered with a smile. He did not mind sharing his hat with Eliot. Rollie figured it kept himself from getting too stuck up. There had been moments during the week when he felt a little proud of himself. Everyone else was proud of him, even his family. When the school had notified the family of his heroic deeds, they had sent a congratulatory reply. Rollie's confidence as a detective had boosted.

Rollie made a point to apologize to Mr. Chad for turning him in. After Disguise class one afternoon he lingered behind until the classroom emptied.

"Hey, detective, something on your mind?" Mr. Chad asked as he combed out the wigs the class had tried on as part of their lesson earlier.

"I just wanted to say sorry," Rollie swallowed, "for getting you arrested."

Mr. Chad waved a hand at him and shrugged. "You thought you were doing the right thing—and it would've been the right thing if I'd been the bad guy. I'm just glad you cleared me!"

"Thanks for catching Enches," said Rollie. "And again, I'm sorry you had to be interrogated by Scotland Yard and all."

"No harm done. And hey, I got a tan from those interrogation lamps, so it wasn't a complete waste of time!"

Rollie laughed. He was so glad to have his favorite teacher back in the clear and back in the classroom teaching.

Eventually Headmaster Yardsly summoned Rollie to his office. On his way downstairs, Rollie bumped into Cecily.

"I was just coming to see what you're up to," she said.

"Headmaster Yardsly wants to see me. I hope he's going to tell me what's in that letter."

"Ooo, me too! Meet me in the Rearranging Library when you're done." Cecily headed downstairs with him.

When he got to the office, Rollie found not only Headmaster Yardsly waiting for him behind his desk, but also Ms. Yardsly. One chair remained empty next to her. Rollie assumed the chair was for him and sat down.

"GOOD EVENING, Rollin," the headmaster boomed in his familiar but alarming way. (He always made Rollie jump.) "We want to share something with you. You've proven yourself very helpful with this case. We'd like you to continue developing your detective skills by assisting us with a new mystery."

"I'll help you with whatever you need, sir," Rollie nodded.

Ms. Katherine E. Yardsly nodded back curtly.

"WELL THEN! We searched Enches' desk and found the other letters you delivered from Mr. Crenshaw. Based on clues we pieced together from the other letters, we learned Herr Zilch still has plans for Sherlock Academy."

"What plans?" asked Rollie.

"Who knows at this point?" The headmaster threw up his hands in clear frustration. "We'd like you to help us watch over the Academy and discover Herr Zilch's next plan."

"Be on your guard, Rollin E. Wilson," Ms. Yardsly drilled in her commanding voice.

"I will." Rollie thought of something. "Have you interrogated Professor Enches? I'm sure he knows where Herr Zilch has escaped to."

Yardsly exchanged a look with his sister. "If you must know, Enches took his own life hours after being arrested. He drank a dose of poison he had smuggled on himself. I'm afraid he's a dead end."

Rollie slumped slightly in his chair.

"Not to worry, Rollin, we'll get another lead on Herr Zilch. But I must issue a word of caution: Zilch and his society are extremely dangerous and devious. You could have been kidnapped or even killed during your confrontation with Enches. While we want you to help keep an eye on things here at school, it would be best to leave the actual chasing of Zilch to Scotland Yard." Headmaster Yardsly shook hands with the boy before he left.

"So? What was in the letter?" Cecily asked as soon as Rollie entered the Rearranging Library.

He joined her by the now-repaired window. "Cecily, this is top secret."

"I'll keep your secret."

Rollie lowered his voice to a whisper. Cecily had to lean in when he said, "Headmaster didn't read me the letter, but he said they've been investigating all the other letters to Professor Enches. Herr Zilch still has plans for Sherlock Academy."

Cecily stared at him, alarm showing in her green eyes.

Rollie continued. "The teachers want us to help watch over the school. Though no one knows what Zilch's next move might be."

Cecily sighed. "Another mystery."

"Can you believe we've solved a *real* mystery already?"

"Well, we *are* detectives after all." Cecily paused and shyly bit her lip. "Rollie?"

"Hmm?"

"What you did was very brave. I would have been terrified to chase after Professor Enches alone."

"I was," Rollie admitted with a slight laugh. "I was relieved when Mr. Chad came to the rescue. What a lucky break!"

Cecily smiled. "That wasn't luck—that was me. I told him what was happening and he took off to help you."

Rollie stared at her with admiration. "See? I knew I needed my Watson."

Cecily nodded and reached down to cuff up the bottoms of her trousers.

"Are those your brother's trousers?" Rollie teased.

"Of course. How did you deduce that, Holmes?" Cecily rolled her eyes and smiled.

Rollie grinned. "Elementary, my dear Watson!"

Epilogue

As always, the weekend came too soon. Rollie loved being at Sherlock Academy so much he actually cared less for weekends. He did enjoy visiting home to see his family, especially Auntie Ei, but he was always antsy to get back to school and his detective classes.

When the hansom stopped next to the Wilson manor, Rollie waved good bye and headed up the front walk way. He paused before going inside.

An envelope addressed to him was taped to his front door. He recognized the handwriting from other letters he had carried. It was from Mr. Crenshaw—though now Rollie could refer to him by his true name: Herr Zilch.

Rollie gulped and tore open the envelope. He got goose bumps as he read the note.

Well done—you saved your school and your great-aunt. Eileen's poisoning is just a taste of what I am capable of doing to your loved ones if you do not stay out of my way. You have no idea of the power I have, or of the scope of M.U.S. You would be wise to drop your pursuit of becoming a detective. This is your one and final warning: do not cross me again, or I will attack those you love in more ways than you can imagine. This is a dangerous game.

Regards,
F.A. Zilch

About the Author

F.C. Shaw started writing stories when she was eight years old. She loves children's stories, Sherlock Holmes, and mysteries, so had to write a book combining all three. She spends her afternoons writing for kids, and her nights dreaming of new stories. She lives with her husband and two sons in a home they have ambitiously dubbed *The Manor* in Santa Maria, California. When she's not plotting stories, she teaches visual arts in local schools and enjoys a good game of Scrabble.

Want F.C. Shaw to come to your school? Contact: schools@futurehousepublishing.com

Connect with the Author!

Say hello to F.C. Shaw here:

www.sherlockacademy.com
www.sherlockacademy.blogspot.com

www.facebook.com/sherlockacademy

@sherlockacademy

@sherlockacademy

Discover more remarkable books from Future House Publishing here:

www.futurehousepublishing.com

www.facebook.com/FutureHousePublishing